NIGHT TRAIN TO NYKØBING
A Novel

Kristjana Gunnars

Night Train to Nykøbing
A Novel

RED DEER COLLEGE PRESS
1998

Red Deer College Press
56 Avenue & 32 Street Box 5005
Red Deer Alberta Canada T4N 5H5

Edited for the Press by Aritha van Herk
Design by cardigan.com
Printed and bound in Canada by Webcom Ltd. for Red Deer College Press

Financial support provided by the Alberta Foundation for the Arts, a beneficiary of
the Lottery Fund of the Government of Alberta, and by the Canada Council, the
Department of Canadian Heritage and Red Deer College.

COMMITTED TO THE DEVELOPMENT OF CULTURE AND THE ARTS

Canadian Cataloguing in Publication Data
Gunnars, Kristjana, 1948 –
Night train to Nykøbing

ISBN 0-88995-187-X

I. Title.
PS8563.U574N52 1998 C813'.54 C98-910477-X
PR9199.3.G793N52 1998

1 3 5 4 2

EAR DEAR JAN. But this is not the greeting that says what I want to say. Inside every greeting there is also a farewell. I try to wrest the good-bye out of the words that mean to greet him. Fully, without reservation. But the word will not go. The farewell inside is waiting to spring out.

Like a cougar. The cougars here have become many. They lurk in the trees. People who pass underneath are suddenly pounced on, taken by surprise. *The Globe and Mail* yesterday listed every cougar attack in British Columbia in the last ten years. They say attacks are becoming more common. The cougar is not friendly. They say you must look it in the eye. You must fight back because the cougar has only one goal. To kill.

Every single household cat in my neighborhood has been killed by a cougar or a bobcat or a lynx. The wild cats prowl the bush behind us and crouch in empty lots still wooded. They prey on the small cats that wander out of doors. At least sixty cats are gone, a kind of ethnic cleansing performed by wild cats on domestic cats.

When I lived in the Okanagan Valley, I had two white cats named Winnie and Pooh. Pooh was eaten by a coyote, or so I thought. Now I think it may have been a cougar. Later I sold Winnie for a hundred and ten thousand dollars to some Cabalarians who had a belief in numbers.

I changed my seat in the first-class compartment so the station would not go out of view when we left. Riding backward, I could see the red brick platform elongate itself as we pulled away. He stood there still as a statue, the man I had just recently risen out of bed with. Hands in pockets, face of stone. The touch of his fingers was still on my breasts. The taste of his kiss. I could still feel him inside me. And yet the train was heading out of Skovshoved Station, severing us. Soon I would see nothing but wheat fields and straw-thatched farms.

My aunt Bodil stood in the hallway in her transparent nylon underpants and white brassiere. She was applying cream to her face in front of the mirror. Her bare feet on the cool parquet floor by the front door. I told her I was coming home again. I was moving back to Copenhagen from Vancouver.

The long sojourn was over now that Québec was going. I said I had come to identify with the Québecois, and when they seceded, I would be without a country again. It was folly to go from one small country to just another small country. To exchange all of Europe, with the European Union, for a paltry bit of the Canada I used to know. I said it was madness to make such a bad exchange.

The heat rises from the ground like an old saying we no longer want to hear. Sunshine fills the air to bursting. I want to drown in that yellow heat. Lie on my deck naked, exposing myself to the harmful rays. I wonder how the day will pass. Why time has become so slow. Nothing stirs. The birds are strangely silent. This morning when I flung open the door to the garden, no birdsong greeted me. Only once did I hear an eagle call from a treetop in the nearby wood. An announcement of carrion, perhaps. A carrion call.

Alain Robbe-Grillet, in *For a New Novel*, says the world has only *one certain quality: the simple fact that it is there. An explanation, whatever it may be, can only be in excess.…* That we imagine everything. That *Drowned in the depth of things, man ultimately no longer even perceives them.* How we color the world with our own desires and aspirations. Everything is contaminated with our longings. Our fears. We invest ourselves in everything we see. *It is, quite simply.*

I think of how I have colored the man at Skovshoved Station, who waited while my train pulled out, with everything I wanted to find in him. That it is impossible to know someone for who he really is. He is always an image of my desire.

Bodil had a small device for rolling her own Prince cigarettes. She pressed the tobacco into a tiny ditch in the mechanism and attached an empty roll of cigarette paper to the end of it. The lid would close and she pushed the tobacco into the empty cylinder of paper. She sat down in the morning with a small tray on her lap, containing tobacco, empty cigarette paper rolls, and the red plastic shuttle. There she sat filling cigarette after cigarette, the day's supply, while the coffee went cold in her cup. I sat down opposite her and watched.

It was her meditative moment. With these scraps of tobacco, she contemplated her family and how she had lost them one by one. How few of us were left. I think she wanted to burn up her sad thoughts. To smoke them out.

From her small apartment in Vanløse, I could hear the noise-makers at eight. The trucks and cleaners and garbage collectors and sidewalk scrapers. A man in a blue cotton uniform that resembled a Maoist pajama set, with a cap on his head, stood across the street with an assortment of brooms and pans. He was cleaning the sidewalk. Down the street the bicycles had begun.

Martin Andersen Nexø was a Danish writer who died in the 1960s. He wrote the novel *Pelle Erobreren*, which was made into the movie *Pelle the Conqueror*. Nexø was a communist. He moved from Denmark to East Germany and lived out his days there. When I came back, he was posthumously made honorary citizen of his birth town, which celebrated its six hundred and fiftieth birthday. It took the Danish authorities over thirty years to get over their author's politics. Or was it just the very idea of preferring East Germany to little Denmark?

In time, I thought, the oddest absurdities may be forgiven. Time always seems to be the conqueror.

Above the brown leather sofa in Bodil's flat was an oil painting. The picture showed a medieval Danish farmstead on the island of Fyn. There was a courtyard of cobblestone. The stuccoed walls were braced by wooden beams. The straw on the roof was held down by crossbeams at the top. The houses were small and low. This was my great great grandfather's farm, when he was a landowner, she said. The old man had a penchant for gambling, but he was not good at it. Because of his gambling, our family lost the farm and went from landowning class to labor class in one generation.

I said we would buy it back. Now that I had returned from Canada, we would go and buy the old farm back and return it to the family. Then we could also say time had conquered that adversity. She looked skeptical. I think she did not believe me. She took some deep, slow drags from her cigarette, and her eyes were fast on me, languorous, almost dreaming.

Yet I had not actually returned, for that was still only a plan. Something in the cards. Written in the tea leaves. Something I saw in the face of the man at Skovshoved Station. His was a beautiful face and in it I could read a volume. Several volumes. Something that said I was about to return. They were penetrating eyes. It was the man who waited with me for the train. The one who held me and I him. The one I would not let go of.

I still had to go back to British Columbia. The house I had constructed was still there. Everything I desired to keep from my life was there, where I left it. A few memories. Pictures, wood carvings, photographs. Piano. Guitar, dulcimer. Fireplace, iron bedstead, empty. They were all there, the roses and hydrangeas, azaleas, and rhododendrons. The hemlocks and maples and cedars still wafted in the breeze off the sea. But somehow the taste of it all was not there. The flavor that kept me happy before was lost. I could not find it.

It occurred to me to wonder if you can lose a happiness because another, greater happiness has supplanted it. Can we not have two happinesses at the same time? Is joy such a jealous emotion that it will not be shared? If so, then the man at the station – whose hair was just beginning to turn white, whose eyes crinkled when he smiled, whose arm I still felt around me – that man had taken too much with him. I did not know what I was leaving behind as I watched him recede farther and farther away on the platform, the hum of the train engine in my ears, the scratch of the steel rails underneath.

No doubt after the death of my mother, I became depressed. Nothing deep or profound, but enough to take away my joys. The little things that make us happy in a day. A carnation in a blue vase, perhaps. Watching *Citizen Kane* again. Or dressing up in red silk so loud that heads turn. Or even a flute sonata or a night at the jazz club. Whatever might have put a happy edge on me before was suddenly gone. Then the man at the station, the one I left there, walked into my life and the color of things altered.

Perhaps it was a thought in the back of my mind as I changed my seat and put a bottle of water on the table in front of me. That he too was dangerous. If losing him meant losing more than what I had already lost. I was led to wonder how deep a depression needs to get before that is no longer what loss is called. And did we both know this about each other?

But even then, I remembered in an unclear way, like you vaguely recall a dream you had, that the home I constructed in British Columbia was the one thing that did give me happiness. A quiet happiness, a whisper without agitation. The sound of a finch or kingfisher or an eagle. The sight of a seal. The flowering of a rose. The sun in the morning. That gave me a very quiet joy, so silent I almost missed it. And then it would all still be there.

So dearest Jan, I begin a hundred times. The beginning is everywhere, like his image. His voice. Annie Dillard says in her book *The Writing Life* that *A writer looking for subjects inquires not after what he loves best, but after what he alone loves at all.* That is how I know he will be standing there for as long as I am writing this. I will continue to see his sad face through the murky train window as we wait to depart. He will walk up to the window and put his hand against the glass where I put mine. Our palms will touch through the glass, as they did that day. The feel of the cold glass will remain on my hand long after.

It is not because I prefer to write about him. To have him in my words like a ghost in my language. A spirit in my alphabet. Not because I choose to. But because he has to be there. As necessarily as there has to be air. As I have to breathe. Without him there, I have no words at all.

My beautiful cousin Kari looked at me across the table. Her long, dark hair spread out from her shoulders. Her hazel-brown eyes focused intently, wide, on me. Yet not on me, but through me. As if I had become the site for surprising sorrows. Her suntanned arms and neck, her long, slender limbs alternately stood and sat restlessly. Around us were scores of posters and prints and objects from the Copenhagen underground. Her garret apartment looked out over other garret apartments, a line of them holding up the horizon.

She showed me her picture. When her daughter Asa was born, the picture she ordered taken. Kari's body lay naked on the floor, spread to the two midwives bending over her. Her face turned sideways in a pain that resembled ecstasy. Her daughter Asa's new head had just emerged in the birthing process. A woman with two heads, one of which was her little daughter's.

I pace the floor. I cannot help the thoughts that lie in the pit of my chest. That I can tell I am going. Like a nomad, I pick up my blanket one more time and head for the sky. The blanket is an old Navajo blanket my mother left me. She had it nailed up on her living room wall. Two square human figures surrounded by a bed of red, ochre and pale violet stripes. A large rug that covered the whole wall. This is the one I take with me now. When I return to him, the one I cannot let go of. I will be there with my mother's Navajo blanket. I have come back home with my only possession.

When the telephone rings at three in the morning, it is as if I am expecting it. Even while asleep, I expect the ring that comes unexpectedly. And he is in a phone booth in Oslo, Norway. I can hear the din of traffic, the city noise. It is noon and I cannot tell what the weather is. I cannot hear any rain. He tells me his love. I hear his words reverberate across the wires. And I am tongue-tied in my bed, wishing to speak, unable to. When the call is over, the silence of the night opens its large mouth. And he, if it is raining, is walking away from the booth, his white trench coat flapping in the wet gust.

Morten, my aunt Trine's husband, stands barefoot in the water of Roskildefjord. He has rolled his loose, black pants with old suspenders to keep them up. His small, shaggy dog wades in and immerses its stomach in the cold sea. Roskilde-fjord beach goes on in a stretch of gray sand and pebbles, laced with the pale green brush of the fields. The water is the color of pewter, glinting like chrome where the sun hits it. Small waves shiver in the fjord, sliced occasionally by a slow sailboat. Morten stands still in the water, facing the outer sea. His long, curved pipe still in his mouth, his left hand supporting the bowl, his now old face still in contemplation. Perhaps he is thinking of himself as suddenly adrift. That when the railroad for which he worked for the last thirty-five years suddenly laid him off, he was without his moorings. He was set adrift. His wife, Trine, stands on the beach in her brown sandals, her navy skirt and blouse, arms on each side, and watches him. She knows he has come loose from his anchor.

The Canadian dawn continues its russet flavor into the morning, the white morning. Tall cedars stand still as if petrified. As if waiting. Not a shred of wind. All seems locked in anticipation. We hardly dare breathe.

I think of him at the station. As he looked back at me through the glass, feet firmly planted on the red brick. His face was clear, but had an edge of something sad. He too was still, as if turned to stone. I wonder now, did we know this about each other? What we know now.

Because of my traveling, I was not on the same schedule as my Aunt Bodil. I woke up at five, the streets outside still dark. I got out of the small, single bed she set up for me in the spare room, out from between the two duvets she lent me. The morning air came in through the open window. I put my slippers on and went into her kitchen. She was asleep in the outer room. I could hear her deep breathing. I quietly scrounged around for filters and coffee beans, made a pot of coffee, and sat down on a stool in the corner to drink it. A community newspaper lay on the side tray. I read the community news. Letters from the neighborhood youths. *We teenagers in Vanløse*, said the letter, *are bored to tears.*

He and I engaged ourselves to each other over the telephone. After. As if we had not realized what lay inside us. It was like the sound of thunder that comes after a flash of lightning. A sound that carries enormous distances. That we had been caught in a current we could not get out of. That we were bound to spiral forward and come to an abrupt resting place. A crash of some kind. An explosion. He spoke calmly on the phone, but he was not calm. *If we do this*, he warned me, *I will be branded a murderer.*

My cousin Kari lived in the artists' quarter of Copenhagen. Rows of brick apartments with tight, sharp gables and high roofs lined the neighborhood. From one gable, you had a view of the next, in succession, one after another. Kari's partner, Anders, had moved to a roof apartment across the street on one side. Her eighteen-year-old son, Njord, had moved to a gable flat on the other side. It was the quarter where all the streets bore Icelandic names. *Gunløgsgade. Njalsgade. Islandsbrygge.* When she looked at me across the room, her big eyes had something wild in them. *Why do they leave you like that?* she was asking. Her son and husband. The three of them were able to see one another through the windows of their three apartments, Kari in the middle.

I insist writers should expose themselves to contradictions, Christa Wolf says in *The Fourth Dimension.* I think it is impossible not to. The way time itself is contradictory. Whenever I look at my watch in British Columbia, I calculate what time it is in Oslo, Norway. What time it is in Copenhagen, Denmark. I live in more than one time zone. They contradict each other. It is both day and night for me. Morning and evening. I am going to work and coming home from work at the same time. My feet trace the fall dust on the street, tiny stones exploding into my shoes as I walk. My feet can feel the pain of glasslike shards pressing against them, my toes facing opposite directions at once.

The red brick of the *perron* had long since receded from view. Perhaps he was now ascending the stairs to the street. Perhaps he was now in the garden, seated in the sun. *I am going to go to the garden,* he told me, *once you are gone. I am going to go there and just sit.*

Because it was a first-class compartment on the train, there was free coffee, mineral water and Tuborg beer in the corner. We could take a drink to our tables. A brown-haired woman in a flowered, cotton dress came into the compartment. She took a beer, a glass, sat down at a table and lit a cigarette. She smoked and drank for ten minutes or so, looking angrily out the window at the landscape of Fyn. Then she stood up and came over to me. *I left my husband at Skovshoved and am meeting my blind mother in Nykøbing,* she said to me. *I seem to be ten crowns short for my fare. Could you give me ten crowns?*

I could see she was riding the rails. One of the destitute who had taken up sponging in first class. Perhaps she rode back and forth all night. *No,* I told her. *I just ran out of everything myself.*

The red-haired doctor had already written the woman's schedule. She sat in his office restlessly, then asked if she could phone her husband. Ten minutes later she returned sobbing. *I'm not going to have an abortion after all,* she wept, gathered her purse and jacket, and went out. The red-haired doctor went out slowly after her. She was standing by the elevator, waiting to go out again into the sooty streets outside Copenhagen Hospital. He went up to her. *Listen,* he said gently, *you are always welcome back here. There is no stigma to your coming back.*

I moved to Edmonton for the winter months to teach classes at the university. Since there was no work to be had in the mountains of British Columbia, it was necessary to go. I had a small flat in the university district that was more like a thoroughfare than a home. People came and went in my apartment. Mealtimes were chaotic and my daily schedule fluctuated wildly.

With my last bit of cash, I bought an essay by Clarise Lispector called *The Stream of Life* at my friend Jodey's bookstore. It was a Tuesday afternoon, warm and windy. The grit off the streets blew in my face when I walked to the bookstore. The air was penetrated by petroleum fumes, car exhaust, and very dry, cream-colored dust. I took the small book home and began to read it. I saw that Clarise Lispector was using the language of ecstasy to talk about being free from love. No longer in love. To fill herself with her own life instead.

I come from the hell of love, but now I am free of you, she writes. The sunshine filled the small room of my flat, and the day was slowly ending. I found suddenly I envied Lispector. I envied her for her freedom. I who was captive.

My Aunt Bodil and I walked back from the Vanløse train station. It was dark already. Lights were on in the small brick houses. The narrow streets were deserted. Only the thoroughfare of Jernbanevej was busy, buses, cyclists, last-minute pedestrians heading home. We came to the yellow brick apartment buildings where she lived. Across the street from her door, we could hear shouting from an open window. A man and a woman argued at the top of their lungs. They were hitting each other, shouting in pain. There were crashing sounds, things breaking.

We stopped on the sidewalk. All about, people had come out onto their balconies to see what was going on. People stuck their heads out of open windows, craning their necks in the direction of the shouting. Some had come outside and stood on the sidewalk in front of the building, smoking cigarettes. As if they were all waiting for something.

We don't have much time, Bodil said to me with quiet determination, *so let's get straight to the point. Tell me about your love life now.* We were sitting on her small balcony facing the park. Below us was the green grass a gardener tended daily in his dark blue, cotton, Maoist uniform. The flower beds were fresh and colorful. Swing sets and picnic tables and a barbecue pit were there, but no one was using them. Farther away, a neat row of clotheslines with clothes hanging to dry. The view of the small park was framed by a series of potted geraniums on the handrail of her balcony. Between us we had a small table, where she had put rye bread and shrimp and Carlsberg beer. It was afternoon.

Her question came as a surprise. I was trying to slake my thirst with a Danish beer. It was very hot. I was seated in the sun, and I could feel a tired drop of sweat forming on my forehead.

In an essay called "On Writing," Eudora Welty says that *We do need to bring to our writing, over and over again, all the abundance we possess.* The excess of our lives. That which flows over. That *jouissance.* I could not help thinking that the abundance of my life was circling him. The one at the station. That bringing my own abundance up in what I write was to bring him into the writing. And it was such a quiet excess. The way he stood so still, as if being pulled by a distant question. A question he could hardly hear, but was trying to listen to beyond the din of squealing train engines and conductors' whistles.

He imposed a silence on us. He said we must not be seen to talk until it was all over. We must leave no voice prints, no fingerprints, no electronic trail. Until it was over.

We had spoken daily for weeks. Mailed each other letters daily, twice a day, three times. *This conversation is really hard to end,* he said on the telephone. It was the last time we talked before our silence. Five in the morning. The streets were wet and glistened in the yellow light of streetlamps in the dark. Lights of the city pinpointed everywhere.

I hung up the phone and looked around the messy room in my flat. I had been too preoccupied to put things away. Papers, magazines, letters, briefcases, and shoes everywhere. A dark, empty feeling had descended. I thought I would have tears, but there was nothing. A stony silence in my chest. And anger. I discovered I was angry.

The image of Thérèse Raquin kept appearing in my mind. At odd moments, in the mornings as dawn broke, in the afternoons as the sun baked the room. Not the face of Thérèse Raquin, which does not exist, but of some actress who played the part in a movie adaptation. Émile Zola's story of two lovers who commit a crime in order to be able to be together. She knows when her lover is committing the crime, when he is drowning her husband. She does not want it to happen, but she does not stop him. She sees it happen and is upset, but she is paralyzed. When it is over, she tries to save the drowned man. When she cannot, she becomes hysterical. Her lover is pleased with her reaction. He finds it a convincing performance. But it is not a performance. She has agreed to something she does not want to see happen. She wants something to happen she knows she cannot live with once it has taken place. Her terrified, paralyzed eyes and hands are what I keep seeing. The hands that instinctively move toward the eyes but never succeed in covering them.

I went back to the town I lived in as a child. The town of Rungsted, north of Copenhagen on the coast. I took my Aunt Bodil with me so I could show her the house. The one we lived in, with the tower on it where I found myself dreaming about my future, looking over the steep roofs of the village. We took the forty-minute train ride and got off at Rungsted Station. When we emerged from the red brick *perron* and found ourselves on the street, I discovered I no longer remembered which direction my old neighborhood was.

We wandered the streets for a while, hoping to run into the house by accident. Whenever we passed a big white stone house, she pointed at it and asked if this might be it. I always had to say no, the tower is missing or the balcony is wrong or the front door was not like that. And always the stained glass window was missing, the big green glass map of Greenland. It was hot. Our feet were tired and sore. We were getting lethargic from the heat. In the end we gave up the search. We made our way to Rungsted Kro, a tavern that had been there for over a hundred years, and sat down in the shade outside. We had a cold beer and a sandwich. It occurred to me that maybe one should not retrace one's steps anyway. That time can only move forward. Time is an arrow. Once it is launched, it cannot turn and go back. An arrow cannot change its destined direction. All it can do is helplessly strike its target.

Let us do something instead that I could not do when we lived here, I suggested. *Let us visit Rungstedlund.* The home of Karen Blixen, which was just around the corner. Because when I was her neighbor, Isak Dinesen was still alive. I could not go and knock on her door then. Now that she was dead, the house was open to the public. In death, she was finally accessible.

Dear Jan. All the aborted letters I can no longer send him. They pile up in my mind like abandoned infants on an island. Suddenly there is no reader. I write into a void where there is no gaze. The milky fog piles in over the town of Edmonton, and I can see nothing but white outside my window. Any sound I might make will be muffled and unheard.

Staring into the fog, I understood I was experiencing our silence in a way we had not intended. As willful cruelty. I found myself wanting my revenge on him. That because I was in love, I wanted revenge.

At that Danish school I attended, all the girls were rounded up into the auditorium. We were told to sit quietly and listen. The village doctor came in to talk to us. He said we must be realistic. It would do us no good to have our heads in the clouds. We must have our wits about us. He took out some rubber contraptions and a diagram of the female reproductive system. He proceeded to show us how to insert a female condom. I was fifteen years old then. I remember paying very close attention. I was not sure exactly how the sheet of rubber was meant to fit, but I memorized every word he said. It seemed very important just then. A matter of life and death to understand what he was saying. *You know perfectly well,* the doctor was telling us, *that men will be men. Men will always be men. Your job is to look after yourselves.*

I knew what I would do in the loneliness of his disappearance. I would take the airplane back to British Columbia. Go to my home in the hills above the water. Build a fire and listen to the rain fall on the roof and the windows. Feel the warmth of the fire spreading all over the room while water poured from the sky outside.

If I thought your affection for me was waning, I would be wild with jealousy, he said. *I would go wild.*

The department I worked for at the university in Edmonton was large. There were over sixty faculty members, and although there was a concerted effort to hire women, two thirds of the department still consisted of men.

There was a party for everyone the day after my last conversation with my lover. I did not know what to do with my newly realized anger. There was no one to send it to. Instead I found myself acting it out. I dressed for the party. I discovered I had put my mind to a certain appearance. A short, black dress, shiny and sleek as leather but soft as mohair. Black stockings and black shoes with heels. I put gentle perfume on my whole body, just enough to be detected without anyone realizing what was being detected. Something in the air.

A colleague sat down on the easy chair armrest beside me. He had come back from the summer looking tanned and spectacular. I asked him what he had done. *Roller blading,* he said. *But I took the wrong turn and fell down.* He showed me his two broken fingers.

We talked about how quickly everyone grows old in this job. How people come to the university youthful and vigorous, and five years later they are old and tired. We agreed the process had to be reversed. Later, when I had my coat on and was leaving, he came up to me in the front hall. *Let's go and get young together,* he said.

I had my party smile. The one I learned after coming to America. I smiled. In my mind I found myself calculating how many times I could go out and hurt my lover. Revenge was so easy. I did not recognize myself. My own thoughts were strangers to me. They appeared like automatized calculations, like numerical problems computing themselves on a screen. Numbers gone insane.

I was thinking of a poster that hung in the mailroom at work. A black and white photo of an attractive woman's face. The bold headlines underneath said, *If you are dressed to kill, make sure he is dressed not to.*

A Slovenian scholar, Slavoj Zizek, was giving lectures at our university. I attended them. The auditorium was packed. He spoke with unusual animation. His arms gesticulated, often with hands spread flat, as if steadying a wobbly person in front of him. Or reaching out to someone with both arms. He often pulled at the left side of his shirt. He told us about a children's book in his country. It was about an island inhabited only by children. On this mythical island, the children sat around discussing all the reasons they were aborted. Why their parents did not want them. It was the island of the aborted.

In my mind you are already my wife, my lover said to me. He spoke with emphasis. Seriousness. As if I needed to understand this or we would be ruined. It was so early still that everything was dark. I was on the sofa in my living room in British Columbia. The many windows glared their blackness at me. The rain pelted down. As he spoke, a storm flared up and the rain beat itself down with extraordinary force. It sounded like war. Like bombs and gunfire and warplanes and explosions. I could hardly hear him. The voice in the receiver was so small.

The worst thing that can happen to a woman, Simone de Beauvoir once said in a radio interview, *is to be in love*. An interview my mother taped and sent me in the mail. I listened to it as I drove in a small red sports car across the Canadian divide. I was pulling up stakes to go and live with my fiancé. When Simone de Beauvoir said that, somewhere close to the Saskatchewan–Manitoba border, I almost turned around. Instinctively my hands turned the wheel toward the shoulder of the road.

She did not have to elaborate. I understood what she was saying. The many ways a woman is taken from herself when she is in love. She accedes. She gives herself over. Her own life has paled and the life of her lover has overtaken her. She pulls up stakes. She forgets.

As it happened, I did turn around. It took a full year, but I did make that u-turn. That was several years ago. Now I look out over the lightening southern horizon. I am keenly aware of the silence of the telephone. There has been no conversation with my lover. I feel the silence like a hole in my chest. Paralyzed by the quiet, with the sound of the city's first cars rushing down the road like a rhythmic accompaniment. I recognize I have been caught again. I hear the voice from the tape again, in memory, exactly the way I first heard it.

On that same road trip, a police car came up behind me, flared its light and sounded its siren, and pulled me over. I could not understand where it had come from. There was no one on that deserted road for a hundred miles in either direction. A young police officer stepped out of the car with a small notepad in his hand. He walked up to my window and looked at me with a smile. I remember thinking he had materialized out of nothing. He told me I was speeding. He fined me seventy-five dollars and said I should slow down.

It occurs to me I should have listened to him. I look for

such emissaries now, but there are none. This time I am alone.

During professional meetings in Hamilton, Ontario, I was put up in a new hotel by the highway. After a full day of meetings, I was tired and went downstairs to a restaurant for dinner. A man I did not notice came in behind me and was also waiting to be seated. The hostess assumed we were together and showed us both the same table. We were about to correct her, but on the spur of the moment decided we might as well keep each other company.

His name was Philippe and he was from Brittany, France. A professor of political science, he was unusually handsome, except for his arms, which had been ruined in the war. We had a conversation that lasted four hours. We did not notice the restaurant had emptied, the place was closed, and the staff was waiting for us to leave.

He told me his wife had recently died. He was in grief. In his inconsolable sorrow, he found himself taking risks he had never taken before. He walked into a street full of heavy traffic. He leaned too far over high balconies. He was careless with his health. It was not conscious, he said. *Somewhere inside me*, he confessed, *I think I must have wanted to die.*

It occurs to me now that I am having the same experience. That I am experiencing my lover's absence as a form of grief. The bare walls, the quiet dawn, the empty hum of an electric gadget still plugged in. That I do not sleep and I do not eat. I go out for a walk in the dry breeze, and five hours later, I am still walking. As if I could walk away his absence.

As day followed day and we did not speak, I understood I was also becoming free. That even if his reasons were good, and I had agreed to his silence, I could only experience that silence as hurtful. Because I was hurt, I could only love him less. *I'm almost free of my mistakes*, writes Clarise Lispector. *I let myself happen.*

On the day I was to leave Copenhagen for Vancouver, I woke up angry. It was a morning flight, and Bodil and I had to get an early start. I did not know why I was angry. I barely touched the breakfast of toasted crumpets and marmalade she gave me. The coffee tasted bad to me. Our conversation was brusque. I answered her questions in monosyllables. That morning I got dressed as though I were dressing for an execution. My skirt and blouse went on grumpily, without care. I pushed everything into my suitcase without folding or straightening, and dumped the bag in the front hall.

My Aunt Bodil did not notice my bad temper. She was admiring my dress, the one I bought on an impulse in Vancouver. She put her hand on the smooth fabric with the white lilies patterned into it. *You can get so many nice things over there*, she said wistfully. Over there, in America.

Slavoj Zizek, the Slovenian lecturer at our university, peppered his talks on Lacanian psychoanalysis with anecdotes from daily life and popular culture. One example he used had to do with the telephone ringing. *Whenever the telephone rings, he told us, I am always worried I will not pick it up in time. I always think that maybe this is The Call. I do not know what this call ought to be, but I am always expecting The Call.*

My dear Jan. There was a time when at least once every morning I would curl up somewhere and weep uncontrollably. I wept without reservation, without self-consciousness, without the guilt that says I am weak and small. I wept because he did not call. Then suddenly one day I had no inclination to break down. I was unmoved. It was a Thursday morning. The cold rain and wind had stopped. It was possible to go out without an umbrella again. I discovered that by some miracle, I had become cold inside.

Even in her fifties, my other aunt, Trine, still behaved like a tomboy. When she walked, her arms were held elbow-out at her side, as though she carried a heavy weight in each hand. She took big steps and her head bent in rhythm with each footfall. She smiled to one side of the mouth, one eye closed, as if in mischief. She said things in a guttural way, making rasping sounds as if it was all too much.

I understood Trine's tomboy behavior was a defense mechanism. I did not know what she thought she was protecting herself against. Perhaps the suspicion that she was weak. Underneath her bluster, she was the least able to cope with distress in the family. When we sat around her wooden table on the deck of her log cabin in the country, she offered us a pile of food. As though riches and generosity were self-evident. She encouraged us to eat aggressively, as though we needed to prepare for a long journey. Mackerel, shrimp, tuna, liver paté, pickled cucumbers, cheeses, all types of rye bread. Wine, coffee.

When we returned to Copenhagen, I said to Bodil that I thought Trine's husband, Morten, was in for a hard time. The one who was retired from the railroad against his will. The one who sat in silence and smoked his crooked pipe while the rest of us chatted. What will happen to Trine if her husband becomes ill? I asked. Men often become ill when they retire. *Oh*, my Aunt Bodil said almost matter-of-factly, without having to give it a moment's thought, *Oh, Trine will not at all be able to cope with that. She will simply fall apart.*

I thought of a French film I had recently seen. About a novelist whose love life is extremely complicated. Her husband has children with another woman. Her lover is married and has children. She herself maintains a childless independence and reserves her privacy for writing. But she cannot help being in love. She has to ask her two men, when they both leave her for the weaker woman, the one with the children, *what is it about love that makes women weak?*

Six-thirty in the morning and it is still pitch dark outside. The town of Edmonton is so far north that I know as the weeks progress it will be later and later before dawn breaks. Soon it will be eight, nine, ten, and still dark. But the blackness allows me to reflect. It seems to me every morning is a new junction in life. What will become of me? It is such an easy question. That I have somehow set things in motion I cannot stop.

On a Saturday I went to my office at work to pick up a student's thesis. I noticed a colleague of mine in another office, bent over a mess of books and papers, sorting them out. I stopped for a chat. He said he could not relax, so he came to work. He had given up his marriage for a woman in Oregon. He accepted early retirement so he could be with her. Now they were having trouble. He did not think the relationship would survive. After all that.

I sat on the chair in his office, my books on my lap, and found I could offer him nothing. No consolation. No cheerful words. He had just described the kind of cruel irony that seems to make up our lives. And fears. He had described my silent fears. The ones that keep me awake at night. What if you miscalculate? What if you design your life in a certain way and then find you have forgotten to factor something in? You were too certain. Your mathematics were not good enough.

It sometimes seems to me that a pestilence has struck the human race in its most distinctive faculty – that is, the use of words, says Italo Calvino in his book *Six Memos for the Next Millenium.* That we flaunt words cheaply. We throw them about for effect until they lose their meaning. *It is a plague afflicting language, revealing itself as a loss of cognition and immediacy, an automatism that tends to level out all expression into the most generic, anonymous, and abstract formulas, to dilute meanings, to blunt the edge of expressiveness....*

I find myself wondering why Italo Calvino is so angry. That he should think we do not know what we mean when we speak. Because inside every word there is another word lurking. A word that has the opposite meaning. That points in the opposite direction. I think it is true, what he says. Yet I cannot help feeling I have never been more sure of the meaning of my words. The words that say I am in love. That I know both meanings are inside what I say, many meanings, opposing each other. It is a full word, *love*. Full of everything we could not say, dared not say, desired to say.

So dear, dear Jan. It is not true that I was angry. That I am angry. That I take my revenge on him. That is not it at all. What is true is that I miss him. Such a simple logic.

My beautiful cousin Kari, with the rich, dark, flowing hair, was a midwife. She went to the Rigshospital every day and talked to pregnant women about birth. She told them birthing is natural. *It is not a disease,* she said. That they should trust their bodies. She helped women deliver naturally. Then one day she came home and was midwife to her cat. Four kittens in a row. After she had rubbed the cat's stomach and all the kittens were out, the mother cat was very attached to her. Whenever Kari came home, the mother cat put its head affectionately in her lap.

She was hoola-hooping in the middle of the floor for the benefit of her young daughter, Asa. She stopped and said to me, *Women in our family have an easy time giving birth. Wasn't it easy for you?*

I am certain of so many things, he wrote, my lover wrote me, *except the one thing: what this is going to do to us.*

We had a date for our return to each other. It was on the calendar, marked by a name for a month and a number for a day. An exact day. There was going to be a precise time on the clock when we would step out of anonymity and into each other's arms. Now I discovered I no longer had the patience I so carefully cultivated before. Time had slowed massively. Time did not seem to pass at all. When I looked at the clock, it was 10:00 A.M. I looked at it again later, and it was still 10:00 A.M.

When this is over I may not be worth having, he wrote.

The train drove onto the ferry, and the massive steel doors shut behind it. I went upstairs to the observation deck. I wanted to see the rain-colored water. The low, pencil line of the island receding. To chart our passage across the water by imprinting it on my visual memory. To see us approach the island of Fyn, where I had told my aunt we would resettle.

But the view was not there. Before us was only a blank sheet of white. As if a mist from the clouds had overtaken the world. I could see nothing.

It was not yet dark. The sun was low in the sky, and everything had a deep glow. A tangerine aura. The train raced through Fyn at high speed. Farmstead after manor after cottage washed by. Long ivory-colored roads stretched through the countryside. A rare automobile, a bicyclist. Fields of wheat, straw-colored and lime green. Homesteads with straw-thatched roofs and crossbeams on top to hold them down. Old farms with courtyards and water pumps, handles protruding into the air. *One of these*, I said to myself, *one of these is ours.*

I knew already then, on the train, that I was being diverted. There was a debate inside my head, but I could not make out the details. The problem of seeing clearly because the familiar face, the quiet, thoughtful expression, the tone of patience in the atmosphere, his pale eyes, superimposed themselves on all the farms of Fyn.

He told me he had many priorities in his life before this, and love was not among them. That now he understood his error. That love was the most important thing. *It is the most important*, he said with emphasis. With finality.

Paula Gunn Allen, a Laguna-Pueblo Indian from New Mexico and professor at UCLA, came to our university to give a course and lecture. I attended the lecture in a massive auditorium packed with people from all over. When Paula Gunn

Allen spoke, her whole body participated. She gesticulated with her shoulders, her hips, she raised one leg behind the other, she walked across the stage. She gave a holistic talk somehow, involving not only the intellect, but our emotions, our sensibilities. In her colorful print dress and curly black hair.

She told us about a certain native writer who had told a story in a novel that should not have been told. A sacred trust of the community was violated when that story was told outside. When you violate that trust, Paula Gunn Allen told us, something very unfortunate is likely to happen to you.

I was thinking perhaps all communities have such codes. Stories that must not be told. That we have to be able to recognize sacred material and not trivialize it. I searched my memory. Have I ever done such a thing? I could not help wondering. Violated an unarticulated code? Walked through it as if it were a translucent cobweb?

At the end of Toni Morrison's novel *Beloved*, the narrator turns the whole world around. After telling so much, she stops. She attests: *It was not a story to pass on.* Since the protagonist's story was best not remembered, *They forgot her like a bad dream.*

It was black night by the time the train neared the end of its journey. While still in the country, there was nothing to see outside the cabin window except my own face. Trying to make out the contours of my ancestral country yielded only the image of myself. It was a tired face. Sad, even. A face filled with the image of a man left behind in Skovshoved. When we came to the city, there were large apartment buildings with lit windows. There were embankments and bridges, rail crossings and highways with headlighted automobiles scuttling about. There were underpasses with lights in them. When we rolled through, black and red and navy graffiti rushed out of the concrete walls with torrid images and desperate words.

The graffiti continued along the walls of the station after I left the train. We all marched through a long corridor to the steps that would take us up to the street and the night life there. An occasional youth could be seen flopped onto the floor, drugged out by something. Coming through the glass doors and out to the pavement, I saw a horde of parked bicycles knotting the passage to the street. People grabbed various bicycles and headed off in all directions.

I walked slowly to Bodil's apartment. I wanted to savor the night air after the long ride in a closed compartment. It was not clear to me how tired I had become. Passing the small brick houses with little gardens around, I could see people settled into their evenings with books or tea or newspapers. Through windows domestic lives became visible. Lights were on inside. Pictures on the walls. Plush furniture. Antiques, decorative plates, even model ships on shelves. There was no one on the street except me. I was thinking of the small bed Bodil had set up for me in the side room. About the pillows and duvets and how I wanted to bury myself in all that eiderdown and forget what had just passed.

But when I walked into my aunt's apartment, I found it was full of people. The living room, the hallway, the bedroom, even. Every chair was taken. On the tables were plates with dinner on them. Meatballs and red cabbage and cucumbers in vinegar. Almond cakes and marzipan chocolates, espresso coffee and liquer. They were engaged in loud conversation. The whole family. They were all there. Cousins and children of cousins, people's former husbands, aunts. All except for those who were dead. Assembled to greet me.

I stood for a moment by the door and tried to collect energy I knew I did not have. It was something I had asked my Aunt Bodil not to do: gather up everybody at once. I said I could not talk to everyone at the same time. But I understood it was like an ocean wave. Something that could not be controlled. If one person knew I was coming, another person would know, and another, until the idea spread, independently of everything else, that someone should be there to greet me. In the end, no one wished to be left out.

Because I was losing my vision, I found an optometry clinic in my university city and had my eyes examined. An attractive young woman in high heels came out and told me she was my new optometrist. In the examination room, she leaned my head back and suddenly stood over me with an eyedropper. *I want to put this dye in your eyes*, she said, *then I can apply this blue light and see what's inside.* She held up an instrument with a blue light pricking at the end of its handle. She told me the dye would freeze the eye and she would be able to see everything inside it.

The yellow dye felt cold and covered both eyes instantly. She put the instrument against her face and peered into my eyeballs with it. I could see the blue light traveling everywhere inside my vision. I could not help worrying about my optometrist. That she would see what I saw. The image I had there all the time would become visible to her with the blue light. She would see my beautiful lover and fall helplessly in love. Because she could not have him, perhaps she would want to throw herself off the bridge. The Highlevel Bridge that lay across the North Saskatchewan River.

The idea that this thought would occur to my optometrist only appeared because it had occurred to me. Since he plunged us into a silence that stipulated we not speak or write or send electronic messages to each other, I did not know what to do. I realized too late it was more than I could bear. But I could not send him a message to say so. This was something I had to endure alone. This silence. This emptiness, where nothing but blank whiteness can be seen through the window.

I took a long walk that led across the high bridge over the river. At the middle, I stopped and looked at the flowing water below. It was not yet icy. The trees along the banks were still lush and green. They had not turned their fall colors yet. I leaned against the railing. I imagined myself dropping the long distance. It had occurred to me that I could not take my revenge on him. I could not hurt him. The only person I could hurt was myself.

Karen Blixen's manor in the town of Rungsted, Rungstedlund, turned out to be a bit like the human brain. Very little of it was in use at any given time. Only a few rooms were available for viewing. The rest was corded off, left untouched, and what had remained of the manor burned down long ago.

We discovered all this on our visit the afternoon I tried to find my old home and failed. Bodil and I arrived at the wrong time. There were no tours through the house just then. But the hostess unlocked the door anyway and told us just to walk through on our own. We took the cotton bags provided to cover our shoes and rambled from room to room. For a large, well-to-do manor, this was a small place. The furniture was frayed and sorry-looking. It was not easy to picture the famous author working there. I imagined she did not write in those rooms.

The door to the courtyard at the end faced south. I knew about this door. About the windows of her study. That Karen Blixen lived her whole life without the man she loved. He was dead. Buried on a hill in Africa. That every evening at sunset, Blixen opened the window facing south and stood silent for fifteen minutes.

I found time had begun to stand still altogether. Time was trapped in the month of September. The end of the month was forever approaching but never arrived. The wind became cold. Frost was in the air. We stepped out and turned our collars up. Everyone expected snow. *Any minute now,* they all said. In this expanded minute that stretched itself for weeks, I had gone from desperation to acceptance to desperation again. I knew what went on inside my days. What I could not bear was not knowing what was happening on the other side. The possibility that something was going wrong. Someone was dead. Maybe murdered. The possibility of anything.

As for the unforeseeable, Clarise Lispector writes, *the next sentence is unforeseeable.* She does not know what the next word is. The next event. Yet she wishes to live inside that darkness. *I don't ask questions,* she says.

I welcome the darkness where the two eyes of that soft panther glow. The darkness is my cultural broth.

But dear, dear Jan. No two words are the same. Lispector writes to the one she is now free of, *I write you because I do not understand myself.* I do not think that is why I write him. These letters that cannot go anywhere. They live and die in the palms of my hands. I write them because I know something about myself. I know how I react to sorrow. The way you begin to understand the actions of a wild animal under stress. A panther, perhaps. How the panther balks once, then again. You know it will draw back every time. It will close down its senses.

Paula Gunn Allen, who was visiting our university, was treated to a departmental dinner after her public lecture. As it happened, I sat beside her at the meal. We talked about our children. She said both her grown children were musicians. When she visited them, she stayed in a hotel. It took too much time, she explained, to clean their places so she could stay there. She saved herself the trouble with a hotel.

It occurred to me we might be miles apart culturally, she and I. She of New Mexico, Pueblo Indian, immersed in what she called the Oral Tradition. And I, of Denmark, with nothing but texts. Written texts. Yet there was this one point on which we were in complete agreement. Our children. We understood each other perfectly as the mothers of our sons and daughters.

Do you want children? he asked out of the blue. For some reason he had left the bed where we lay and was returning again. Coming toward me. It was a hot night. I had thrown the covers off, the blanket and sheet onto the floor, and hoped the breeze from the open window would cool down my naked skin. It was an unexpected question. Out of context. His question so surprised me that I forgot he was coming toward me. There were still people out on the streets. I could hear them through the open window. Streets of this Danish town that, for some reason, did not sleep.

The woman had no feelings going into this. She bunched up the pillow under her head to make herself comfortable. Everyone had gone away. She was alone in the small, white-walled room. The husband went home to breakfast. The mother-in-law was already back at the house, cooking. The nurses took their break. The doctor went home for breakfast too. She took a book out of her bag and started to read. John Steinbeck, *The Grapes of Wrath*. Everywhere in the opening scene, red dust filled all nooks and crannies. Red dust lay in people's eyelids, in their shoes, on the potatoes they ate for dinner. The air was red with dust.

There was no pain, no labor, nothing. They said it would take hours. But when a nurse walked by accidentally, she noticed what was happening. Suddenly everyone was summoned. People in green shirts came and rolled her into the delivery room, her novel still hanging from her fingers, pages flying as they rushed down the hall. The woman did not understand everyone's panic. Nothing was happening. But oddly enough, even though she felt nothing, there was a baby. The doctor rushed into the room in time to receive it. He held the infant high up in the air where she could see it. Like a grail of some sort. He called to her, *Look what you got*.

The woman looked at this infant, whom she had not exactly expected. Almost instantly she was overcome by some invisible cloud. She began to cry. Once begun, she could not stop.

My cousin Kari's son, Njord, was now a handsome and tall young man of eighteen. He was slim and tanned, his light brown hair tied in a pony tail. I sat down beside him the night I returned to Bodil's flat from the train station and found everyone gathered there. I took a few bites of food and listened to them talk.

Njord's impulsive mother once took off to New York without warning or planning. She took her young son along. Kari insisted she simply wanted to see New York with her own eyes. It was Njord's only visit to America. Since I had just come from there, he wanted to tell me his personal impression of America. *In New York,* he told me with grave enthusiasm, *everyone was shooting everyone else left and right.*

Jeremy, my roller-blading colleague, who had asked me if we could go and get young together, was leaning against an espresso stand on campus. He was wearing a three-piece suit in gray-green and appeared very official. As I walked by, I stopped and asked him why he was dressed up. He was serene-looking that day. It occurred to me he always did look serene. In control. *Because I'm going to a funeral,* he answered without a touch of emotion.

Send me your picture, my lover asked me on the phone, *just to have with me while this is going on.* I promised him I would. But a month went by and I had not yet done it. The picture I had of him, the one I took myself under a tree in Denmark that caught him unawares, was on my nightstand. But after he imposed silence on us, I banished his photograph. I took the picture in its frame and placed it upside down in my desk drawer. Then I refused to indulge him by sending him mine.

It occurred to me if words were not allowed, I could use other signs. My friend Mikel, who was a photographer, came to my flat with her camera and we mapped out a strategy. We went to the room with the swimming pool. On the blue-tiled poolroom wall there hung a bright red lifesaver ring. The kind you throw out to people who are drowning. I positioned myself next to the rescue device. A red circle leaping out of the blue wall. Mikel took the pictures. Will he understand? I asked her. She could not know. I knew she had no way of knowing.

But it was my colleague Jeremy who offered to come to my rescue first. Because I had stopped by the espresso stand on a day when I found it hard to conceal the despair I felt. He asked how I was. A rhetorical question we ask each other, to which we do not expect an answer. So I gave him no answer. But that day I had been holding back tears in the middle of all my duties. Before a class of forty-two students, I held back tears. During consultations with thesis writers. During a committee meeting, my reticence almost noticeable. My colleague noticed. *Look*, he said by way of answer for me, *I have just the solution for you.*

My mother requested, before she died, that we not have a memorial service for her. Instead we should have a party at her house. On the afternoon of her burial, we opened the big, old house up to the people of the town. There was plenty of food and drink. The house was packed with people. They came from all directions. From faraway cities. We played the music she loved on the piano. We read the poems she cherished. Carl Nielsen and Rabindranath Tagore. We tried to do what she asked of us: to have a good time.

But I could see we were a sad bunch. There was a cloud of wrath over the whole house. Underneath the sweet and consoling demeanor, everyone there was in shock. This was not supposed to happen, we seemed to say when we looked at one another. This could not have been in the cards. Reality took a wrong turn, we insinuated. It was evident to me, even at that early moment, that what we had in the passing of my mother was a genuine loss. We looked around and realized we did not know what to do without her now.

In the middle of the celebration, I fell into the arms of a big woman who had helped with the care-giving. I sobbed uncontrollably and deeply. Never in my life had I sobbed like that before. Not even as a baby.

It was my son who suddenly stood there like the only strong pillar the family had left. He suggested a solution for me. He said we should go and see the Dalai Lama.

One day in Copenhagen, I woke up unusually late. It was already daylight and the gray walls of the room looked matte and clean. Through the gauze curtain draped against the open window, street noises sounded. A delivery truck. The scraping of a street broom. The swishing of bicycle tires. I could tell it was overcast. The voice of a radio announcer could be heard through the closed door. Bodil was no doubt up, listening to the morning program on Radio Copenhagen. The peculiar city accent of the announcer sounded striking just then. I crawled out from under the duvet and put on a robe my aunt had left hanging on the front door hook. When I walked into the foyer and looked down into the living room, she was there. Bodil, seated in her black leather chair, head cocked slightly to the right as if to hear better. Rolling her cigarettes.

The Dalai Lama did not just come into the hall. He arrived preceded by a number of monks and followed by a number of monks. All of the devotees wore maroon-colored robes. They had their beads and strings. The teacher himself wore ochre yellow and maroon, one shoulder left naked. He sat on a low chair in the center of the podium, all his disciples settled around him. My son had found me a good seat close by. I could follow every move the teacher made. His every breath. It occurred to me then, as it had often before, as he prayed and chanted before speaking, that if Jesus Christ were back now, he would be very much like the Dalai Lama.

The teacher spoke in a deep, sonorous voice. Everything he said was crystal clear. He summarized over two thousand years of complex Buddhist teachings into phrases that rang pure as spring water. *Once it has begun,* he was telling us, *it is very difficult to alter the course a certain Karma has taken.*

Dear, dear Jan. I want to tell him I am not here. That I have left my body and am spinning in the spheres somewhere. I have turned into a vibration of sound and cannot be found. I am everywhere at once. My feet do not come down anywhere because there are no feet. Love did this. I want to tell him about this transformation, but he cannot hear. He is unable to hear because I am no longer human. The sound I make cannot reach the human ear.

All of a sudden a door was thrown open through which life came in, says the Steppenwolf in Hermann Hesse's novel *Steppenwolf.*

You have a dimension too many, Hermine says to him. *Whoever wants music instead of noise, joy instead of pleasure, soul instead of gold, creative work instead of business, passion instead of foolery, finds no home in this trivial world of ours.*

One late afternoon at my Aunt Trine's log cabin in northern Sjælland, I became tired. We had wandered along the Roskildefjord coast for hours, through the wheat fields, the woods, along the beach. We had stood in front of the pale ocean and sat on the white rocks. But when we returned to the house, I realized the last days were weighing me down.

I lay down for a nap in the extra bedroom. This was where Trine's son, my cousin Niels Eric, lived when he was home. Lying on the hard wooden bed that had no mattress, I looked at the bare log walls of the room. The wooden cabinet against the wall, unpainted. Not a sign of my cousin was in the room. Not a single memento, personal object, item of clothing that might be his. It was as if he did not exist. It occurred to me to wonder where his place was. He was the cousin I had never met. Not once, even though we had both been alive for over thirty years. He was a rumor to me. A story told of a tall, blond fellow in wooden shoes who gardened for a living and hiked through the countryside on weekends and managed to pay his parents a visit on occasion. When he did, it was rumored he lay down on their sofa and slept the visit through.

In his novel *Snow Falling on Cedars*, David Guterson calls *the art of waiting over an extended period of time – a deliberately controlled hysteria.* . . .

But as the days progressed from cold to warm again, to Indian summer and back, I found there were cracks in that control. That the hysteria peculiar to lovers, to lovers who have to wait, began to leak. The seeping of one world into another suddenly showed up in my work, my thoughts, my body. I became disorganized. Forgot to answer letters, reply to messages. Forgot to think thoughts to the end. Subsisted on fractured, fragmented conversation. Then I found my private hysteria had invaded my body like a disease I could not prevent. All my nerves were buzzing. My muscles were on edge. I was shaking. Even my bones were shaking.

I realized something had to be done. But I did not know what I should be doing.

I stood in the mail room at work, facing the mailboxes. My back was to the room. Something in my mailbox attracted my attention, so I stood reading it. I did not turn around, but I could sense the presence of someone behind me. Someone in the room. When I did turn around, I saw it was my colleague Jeremy. The one with the solution, he said, to my problems, whatever they were. He was standing very still by the door. His clear face showed no expression. Glasses shielded his eyes. He wore an immaculately pressed suit and a very slight, overconfident smile.

The slowness of time became harder to take. The days lumbered forward. When the weather was good, the whole town was out on the streets. People walking, sauntering, sitting on terrace cafés on Whyte Avenue. Hiking briskly through the river valley parkways. Bicycling with helmets on. It seemed everyone but me was engaged in the day. I had found myself out of focus. Somehow I was not there. Out to dinner with friends, out walking with friends, in the middle of conversations with friends, I discovered I was somewhere else. Disengaged.

In this core I have the strange impression that I don't belong to the human race, Clarise Lispector writes.

Hovedbanegaarden, the main train terminal in Copenhagen, was larger, busier, and dirtier than what I was used to. People rushed forward on both sides of the station, milling through like water. Some just sauntered, often foreigners looking for something. People filed through the kiosks, the magazine stands and cigarette stands, piling up the newspapers for journeys ahead. *Berlingske Tiderne. Aftenavisen.* A couple of cafés were enclosed behind glass partitions to give the illusion they were separate spaces. People had coffee there in the middle of a thoroughfare, the tables still full of napkins and used cups from former customers. In the very clean public toilets below, the purple lights were so low it was almost impossible to see. The attendant sat on guard behind a glass window, dispensing soaps, tampons, underwear. It was to discourage the use of drugs that people had to tend their affairs in darkness.

The whole station, it seemed to me, was a terminal for much more than trains. It was an exchange center for the underground. The nether world that milled about on the surface, disintegrating itself in the illusion of invisibility. I had come in on the Skovshoved connection. I bought a ticket at the wicket in the terminal and found the *perron* with the number for Nykøbing. Track number fifteen.

The Call came unexpectedly at five-thirty on a Thursday morning. I was up reading *Snow Falling on Cedars*. Often I lost concentration and looked out the big window. It was still dark. The lights of the city sparkled like waves on water caught by sun. City lights went on as far into the south and east as I could see. There was the constant pain in my heart I had become used to. The hollow place in my chest. The need to pray this time would end – and the inability to do so. The sense of futility.

His voice was clear but the surroundings were noisy. Crowds could be heard milling, shouting. The sound of loud motors. A loudspeaker blared into the receiver, crowding out his voice. *I will run out of time in three minutes,* he said. He had to speak. Had to call. He was in the airport in Trondheim. A brand new terminal, glinting with the clatter of travel. He had found a phone in a corner. He sat with his back to the world, his forehead pressed against the glass and his hand covering one ear.

Anything you do not give freely and abundantly becomes lost to you, Annie Dillard says in *The Writing Life. You open your safe and find ashes.*

It occurred to me this giving had become my life. Something so unnoticeable I could hardly tell it was there. A transferal of my energy to him, the one who received whatever I had to give. Just so this part of me would not be lost, but instead inhabit him where he went. Across the street, into the store, at a meeting, in front of his desk. Everywhere he went, there was that which I had given him.

Something I could not tell him during that hurried phone call from the Trondheim airport. That on some level, a space hardly discernible, he called too late. Something had passed from the scene. That I answered with only the remnants of myself. That I was no longer in my own possession.

I returned to my home in the mountains of British Columbia to think things over. It was important to take the time, the space, to find out what had happened. In what sense I was lost from myself. I flew over the Rocky Mountains and found it was raining in Vancouver. The long bus ride had standing room only. People packed themselves into the bus, crowded into the back and dozens more filed in through the front door. Finally the driver had to deny waiting passengers access. He told them to wait half an hour for the next bus. The ferry plowed through Howe Sound, made choppy by wind and misty by rain. We could not see the coast on the other side. The islands along the way were half hidden from view. On the other side, there was no bus and stranded passengers stood looking helpless in the terminal.

Clarise Lispector writes about a dream she had. In the dream, many people obeyed a soft drink advertisement. The ad was stronger than they were. She says it was a dream about *automatic people acutely and solemnly aware that they are automatic and there's no escape.*

I put the book down on the ottoman and looked out the window. There was a full moon sliding over the skyscrapers in the southwest. I thought I knew exactly what I was afraid of. That I too was in the process of becoming automatic. Going to work, to the office, obeying orders, filling in my evenings with small entertainments, getting by. Reducing the flow of emotions, so I would not recoil over feelings like Lispector's oysters do when lemon juice is squeezed on them.

On our meeting in the mail room, my colleague Jeremy invited me to come home with him for tea. It was the hour between the workday and dinner. Late afternoon. The sun is low in the sky. The light has paled and become flat. He said his invitation was not an advance on my person. Just a friendly tea and a solution. I relented. It was not difficult. We closed up our offices and drove away in his newly purchased gray Toyota. The car still had that new smell.

Jeremy's flat was in a high-rise on the corner of One-hundredth Street and Saskatchewan Drive, by the river. He had the place furnished in black and chrome, modernist objects of leather and glass. It seemed in character, the place and the man. He actually did make tea, a kind of Earl Grey mixed with fennel. The hour between four and five in the day stretches and slows. I watched the view from his window and could feel the time lengthening while lights began to come on in the downtown tall buildings. One by one, small squares of light suddenly turned on.

Jeremy was talking, but I was not listening. I heard the words, but nothing really registered. He could tell but kept talking anyway. I heard him say he understood something difficult was going on. He would not ask the details. He knew it was personal. But there is something that is preferable to jumping in the river, he said. I did not know what he meant. I looked at him quizzically. It was then I noticed him unwrapping a diabetic kit. A small, plastic box that contained a device for reading blood sugar levels, something to prick the finger with, a small bottle of insulin, and disposable hypodermic needles.

I telephoned my Aunt Bodil to let her know when I was coming back. The airplane ticket was already in my purse. She was happy to hear the date was set. Her voice was sweet. She told me she was having trouble with her daughter, my cousin Kari. For months, Kari had been scolding her mother, angry with her for things Bodil did not understand. For things done in the past she did not remember. *I think she is fictionalizing all this,* Bodil said to me. *She is making it all up.* I did not know what to say.

Why do your children all of a sudden turn against you? she asked in genuine confusion.

My dear Jan. We began to speak again. But not like before. What was deprivation became excess. Every chance we had, at any hour, every day. Often at night. At work. At home. Between us lay half a century of things we did not know. Or if we knew them, they were things we had to learn again.

The first snow fell in my university city. The roads were iced over. Snowflakes mixed with hail fell harshly on the windowpane, the railing, the branches of naked trees. I was oblivious to this new winter. The wind blew corns of ice into my face, and I did not notice. I did not know how to make the time pass faster, so the day would arrive when I was in his arms again. I looked at the white light of noon, and the universe seemed frozen in place. A world of cold days that refused to give my lover to me.

I miss you something awful, he said on the telephone. There was an echo on the line.

The Norwegian writer Sissel Lie was touring Canada. When she came to my city, I was her host. I took her to dinner, to lunch, to see the town, to a friend's house. We went for tea at the Highlevel Diner. She read from her books with dramatic intonation. With her short, gray hair, her gray jacket and black slacks, she presented an androgynous profile. Her left hand was often in her pants pocket while she held the book up with her right.

I read her first novel before we met. The book was charged with sexuality and eroticism. *Lion's Heart* it was called. In the novel, two women have an erotic relationship. A man and a woman also do. A wife and her faithless husband do, but separately. A man and two women do, in a Renaissance bed, limbs and tongues intertwining, bodies sliding over other bodies. I asked her why she inundated her novel with so much sexuality. She was unhesitant. *Sex is the most important thing in life*, she said, her cup of Earl Grey tea halfway in the air.

Why is it that an instant before things happen they seem to have already happened? asks Clarise Lispector. In a flash, you see your fate laid out before you. You hear the door slam before it does. You hear the phone ring before it rings. You see your lover reach for you before he is your lover. I recognized what Lispector was saying. It was not a surprise to me that this man, who the day before was unknown to me, today put his arm around me. This evening reached over and kissed me on the lips.

How everything that happened afterward was already known to me. His movements, people he spoke to, what he had for supper. Everything he did was as familiar to me as what I did myself. At the same time, I knew nothing, and I knew I knew nothing.

In my own life, the one I led before, I had bought a house in the country. A place far away from where I worked and where I carried on social and professional obligations. In this other home, my real home I called it, there was nothing to press me in any direction. Just silver beaches glinting like chrome and mountains of ochre and rust-colored maple leaves on the ground in the fall. This home existed for me so I would not lose myself. I never want to lose myself again, I decided when I moved there.

On the Remembrance Day weekend, I went back to British Columbia. The ferry was just leaving when I drove my Jeep down the hill and was the last vehicle on board. The rain clouds over Vancouver parted when we reached the Sunshine Coast, and I drove home with streams of sunlight falling on the green trees and grass. Back at my university city, the ground was covered in snow and patches of ice, and the wind blew flurries of snow dust on street corners.

When I came home, I turned the heat on, read my mail, opened the curtains to let the sun in, and put his photograph on my desk. It was disconcerting. I felt dislocated. Coming home was not the same any more. My delight in the sea and mountains around was not there. My relief at being home was gone. The telephone rang ten minutes after I arrived. It was my lover, wishing me a welcome back to my house. But I did not like what had happened. For the first time, I did not want to talk to him. I realized that in spite of all my efforts not to, I had lost myself.

That I had lost my head. I was compromised when I had committed to a lifestyle where I would not be. My own life, my own decisions, my own schedule. But now I found myself at the mercy of another's. His life, his decisions, his schedule. The clock went from four to five to six. By seven the dawn was in. A pastel white and crimson light lay over the hills. Clouds hovered low, touching the white water. The branches of tall cedars spread perfectly still in the morning calm. Yellow and brown leaves of maple trees. Withering leaves of alders, half-eaten by autumn rains. I knew as I once again watched the splendor of the country morning that with everything my lover and I had set in motion, I was nonetheless planning to do something I could not do. He would in the end be waiting in some premeditated location, and I would not be there.

The Danish writer Michael Larsen came to give talks and readings at our university. Since my schedule conflicted and I could not attend, I agreed to take him to lunch instead. We went to a Korean restaurant on campus. He had a beer and lentil soup. He chain-smoked and gave off the air of having lived hard. His straw-blond hair was cut short, his cheeks ruddy. He told about being a film critic covering the festival at Cannes. How he and the photographer sent with him drank and partied all night,

slept it off on the beach, and woke up in the sunshine with people all around, children playing, balls bouncing by.

He said he lived alone with his dog in a country house in
northern Sjælland, near Gilleleje. I confessed I had in mind the
same situation and had been looking on Fyn. As I told him
this, I wondered why some writers absent themselves from
society like that. Why it becomes so important to go away, into
the countryside by yourself, when what you do in life is write.
It dawned on me at that moment that I did not know anymore
whether I was moving back there because I wanted to go home
or because I was following my lover and leaving myself.

Michael Larsen was on a reading tour of Canada. He did not
know the country and had been given a schedule of events by
the Danish embassy in Ottawa. He came to my office and we
studied his schedule. I told him the itinerary was crazy. It was
trips like that, concocted by bureaucrats in Ottawa who did
not have to go on them, that killed authors. I said I had a
schedule like that once, and it was the last time I did a reading tour. Forever after, I said no to tours. He looked at me
slightly alarmed. His ocean-blue eyes were obviously lost in
reflection. *I will never do this again either*, he said, shaking his
head, holding his lit cigarette in his left hand.

In the late afternoon, when the sun was low and the maple
leaves became coral red, I sat down at the big gray pinewood
table that served as a dining table. The chairs were large

pinewood stools with high backs, painted dark, moss green. They were hard to sit on, and the table had lines and grooves chiseled into the top. On the table I placed a blank sheet of paper. I pulled out a ball-point pen from the pencil container, a ceramic mug I once bought in the city where I work. I traced a line down the middle of the paper. On one side I wrote "what's right"; on the other side, "what's wrong." This way, I thought, I could systematically figure out what to do in my life.

I found many things wrong with the relationship between me and the man I was addicted to. The one I spoke to every day on the telephone. Whom I wrote to. Whose letters and phone calls came in once, twice, three times daily. Often. I discovered there were more things wrong than there were right. I had to weigh one item against another and I could not. I tried to establish a list of priorities. I soon realized that the difference between one priority and another may only be one of degree. There were some things that could not be balanced. Or compared. How could I compare the act of writing with my child? My own happiness with his? Risk against certainty?

I searched for something ultimate. In an essay by Hélène Cixous on Clarise Lispector, titled "Clarise Lispector: The Approach," I found something I thought I could hang on to. Cixous wrote: *We have only to love, be on the lookout for love, and all the riches are entrusted to us. Attention is the key.* I could not help wondering where Cixous, and even Lispector, got this certainty from. How could they be so sure? And what should I pay attention to in that case? Everything? Love itself? Would I know it if I saw it?

I did not think I would recognize love. Even if it called me at four in the afternoon and declared itself.

The blue upholstered seats in the general compartment of the night train were comfortable. There were not many people in my car. The table between seats was large and useful. I had evening coffee and looked at what had become darkness outside. Nothing to see except the occasional farmstead lights.

I was joined by a young woman and her child, who seated themselves opposite me. A boy of about two years who walked in the aisle on short, stubby legs and crawled up and down the double seat that contained his mother. The woman was a picture from a fairy tale. Her long blonde curls went in every direction. Her long cotton dress suggested romantic domesticity. She had a perpetual smile and an air of gentleness about her. The child spent most of the ride eating. Every time his mother put a bite of food on the table, an apple or a sandwich, the boy ate it up. Carrots, crackers, cheese. After an hour of this, I began to wonder. Was there room in that small body for all that food? The child was an eating machine.

The woman woke up in a roadside motel in Red Deer, Alberta. It was 6:00 A.M. The brown and orange fifties-style furniture stood dark and depressing around the room. Outside on the highway, huge oil trucks and cargo vans rumbled past. The woman was on a lecture tour and was scheduled to speak to a college audience at 9:00 A.M.

She discovered she had awoken to severe abdominal pain. Her body was cramped up and she could not move. The only thing she had ever experienced that resembled this pain was being in labor. Labor pains. She tried to stand up but could not. She ended up crouched on the floor by the bed, where she tried to put her feet. There was a telephone on the nightstand. From the heap she was in, she reached for the receiver and managed to dial the number of her friend Arnold. When he answered, she only managed to blurt out that he should come and take her to the hospital. *Hurry*, she said.

Arnold arrived after what seemed like an eternity. The woman managed to put her jeans and shirt on, and they went to his car. He had to hold her up while one wave of cramping after another shot through her.

At the emergency ward, the receptionist's desk stood imposing and large. The intention was for patients to sit down and register themselves, give their names and health care numbers. Instead, the woman threw herself on the counter in front of the receptionist. *Help me*, she whispered. Then she blacked out and came to on a stretcher in an examination room. There she lay for four hours, the pain that most resembled labor holding on to her.

The woman was examined by three different doctors. She was wheeled into the ultrasound room, and two doctors rolled a little ball over her abdomen. After being back in the examination room for what seemed like a long time, in and out of consciousness, miraculously the pain left her. She lay like a ruin after the flames have been put out. In the end they told her they could not find the fetus she had apparently miscarried.

Ours is the century of unreason, the stamp of our behavior is violence or isolation, writes Eudora Welty in an essay on Jane Austen. *Non-meaning is looked upon with some solemnity.*

It occurs to me Eudora Welty has described my life. The inevitable twentieth-century life. Life at the end of the millennium. Whatever the next century may bring, I cannot but wonder if this combination of violence and isolation can be surpassed.

That I find myself in a tower above the city in the dead of night. The lights outside seem to blink as the currents of cold air pass between me and them. Streetlamps glow yellow all along the main avenue that stretches from my window to the horizon in the south. Behind me is the blank telephone. The memory of ringing the night before. That the voice on the other end was a voice of desperate ecstasy. And the knowledge that around him and me, whole worlds were crumbling.

I'm making myself, writes Clarise Lispector. *I'll make myself until I reach the core.*

As if there were a core in us. Up to now it seemed to me I had only experienced the self as a fluctuating puff of steam. The kind that blows off the train as it sets out from the station.

We stood in each other's arms on the platform, waiting for the train. It was a last good-bye. A solitude lay around each of us, shielding us from what would have been sorrow. It was not sorrow. His arms tight around my waist, my back. My arms enveloped his shoulders, his neck. His cheek rested against mine. I could feel the cheekbone, the forehead, as though they were my own. He was thoughtful. As if there were something more to think about. I was not. I was simply taking the evening train. It was my intention to travel into the night and into my life.

In the middle of November I found myself in Normandy, France. At the Castle in Caen, as part of a small group of Nordic writers in town to talk about Nordic writing. It was alternately rainy and sunny. The narrow streets crisscrossed one another, packed tightly with boutiques selling lingerie, coffee, pastries, books, and high fashion. Antique stores crammed the sidewalks, and cafés stayed open. Inside people sat alone at small tables, smoking and lingering, in what appeared to be serious thought.

At the banquet in the Castle on a Saturday night, my companion was the Icelandic writer Gudbergur Bergsson. His latest novel, *The Swan*, was attracting much attention in France. Milan Kundera had recently written a glowing article on the book. It was said Bergsson had written the book of the decade.

Gudbergur was a tall, handsome man with slightly graying hair and a modest, if not shy, demeanor. He was overly reserved, and absented himself from most occasions. Over dinner he told me he had seen me cross the street of Tjarnargata in Reykjavík nine years ago. He told me what I had been wearing, whom I had been with, and exactly how I had moved around the corner. I said he seemed to have an extraordinary memory. *Yes*, he told me, *at that time I was so sensitive, I remembered everything I ever saw*. When he looked at me across the table, his eyes were large and sad. The expression on his face was intense and seemed to say he had reason to be overly sensitive. I could not help thinking this must be how you look at a dinner companion you have decided to trust, if you have been abused earlier in life.

After our stay at the Castle in Caen, I took the 8:00 P.M. train to St. Lazarre. My cousin Thorir rode back with me. Thorir was such a good-looking man that people stopped what they were doing when he appeared. His perpetual smile drew people to him like a magnet. His casual demeanor made him seem comfortable in the world.

On the ride home we shared a first-class compartment. He bought us each a Heineken, and we sat down to catch up on family history. We told each other what had happened over the years. His brother was an actor in Paris. His sister, he said, disappeared. She was nineteen. It was ten years ago. She was depressed and her counselor advised she go to school in Norway, near Sognefjorden. She went, but during the winter she wrote a good-bye note and then disappeared. Eventually the whole family was in Sognefjorden looking for her. They never found her. In the end it was assumed she had drowned herself.

I asked Thorir what could have made her do that. He sat with his elbows on his knees and looked at the floor. Then he looked me straight in the eye. *She was in love with a boy*, he said, *and he rejected her*.

My dear dear Jan. Missives that do not reach him. Thoughts that contain everything I know about him. How they cannot travel. Like orphans, they return to me. To my own fingers.

What he wanted from me. To reach into me and find something he did not have. As if my body contained the missing ruby. His naked body tightly against mine. His ardent love. The way he whispered my name to me as he loved me. As if my name were a revelation. *You are a revelation,* he said.

It was nearly eleven at night when we reached St. Lazarre. The wind was blowing rain-filled gusts in circles at the station. Thorir stood in the taxi line with me for a while. We parted with a handshake. It had been a topic of conversation in Caen, how different cultures construe different modes of parting. In France it is a kiss on each cheek. In Norway it is a warm hug. In Iceland it is a handshake. I got in a cab and made my way to a tiny hotel in the rue de l'Annonciation.

The hotel room was cold and barren. No pictures on the wall, no decoration. Just two single beds next to each other, a desk, and a telephone on the wall. When I took the receiver off the phone, the whole machine came loose and almost fell off the wall. I turned the heaters on. While I waited for the room to warm up, I tried to call my lover in Oslo. The lines to Norway were busy. I tried several times. I still had my coat and boots on, for the room was chilly. I could feel a certain anxiety crawling up my spine every time I heard the busy signal.

Outside were the rooftops and courtyards of central Paris. Flower beds hung in unlikely places along backyard walls. Chimneys stood up like sentinels.

About the city that night, diesel-fueled trucks were parked everywhere, blocking traffic in and out of town. Truck drivers were on strike. They parked their trucks across the road, turned the lights off, and left them there as roadblocks all night. The news reached me that just a bit earlier, a sedan full of teenage boys tore into the roadblock. The boys wanted to get home. They were impatient. They took down the wooden barricades on the highway, got back into the car and sped down the road into Paris. They did not see the truck parked across the road. There were no lights. In the fury of their driving, they crashed into the truck. All the boys died.

He told me we could not meet again till it was over. That I had to wait. I did not know exactly what I was waiting on. I had to trust him. Put faith in what I did not know. Except that someone would be harmed, and I did not know who it was.

I counted the days till I would see him. Every morning I resumed the count as if for the first time. How many days left. I looked at the calendar once again, as if it were a stranger, and I had to decipher its hieroglyphics. Even now, alone in a cold hotel room in Paris, my black laced boots on my feet, still wearing the brown, knee-length velvet jacket I bought in Caen. Sitting on the edge of the thin bed with a telephone receiver in my hand. I could hear the beeps of the busy overseas line. I was counting days. The sense of isolation and helplessness seemed to emanate from the white walls of the room. I tried to keep the involuntary tears inside my eyes. Then I thought it did not matter. No one would care whether or not I wept in a small room in the rue de l'Annonciation.

The terrible duty, writes Clarise Lispector, *is that of going all the way to the end.*

It had not occurred to me until this moment that I would need to stay till the end. An ending I could not imagine, yet I should wait for it.

By the end of the school term I found everything in a strange kind of shambles. By seven in the evening, I collapsed with fatigue and slept until two. I got up in the middle of the night as if it were morning. Much of the city was still up. The last cars were plowing the roads with people getting home from parties. I made a pot of coffee and wondered again what was happening to me. There were all my projects lying about the apartment in pieces. Unfinished. It was clear to me that something valuable was gone. The ability to carry on uninterrupted. To finish what I started. To see things through. Where did it go?

In the beauty salon on Whyte Avenue, a very young woman cut my hair. Young men wearing costume jewelry and young women in black ran back and forth. While I waited I fingered a magazine. The kind of magazine put out for the young and the restless. Inside there was an advertisement for a Champs Élysées perfume. There was a black and white photograph of the Champs Élysées in Paris. It was night and it was raining. The picture was blurry. Many cars were heading down the avenue with lights on. The caption said, *If you let your spirit free, where would it go?*

It was while I was in Paris that André Malraux was interred in the Parthenon. The ceremony was at night. The Parthenon was lit up to blaze magnificently in the black drizzle. People thronged the sides of the avenue and crowded around the square. Plexiglas covers had been constructed so the dignitaries would not get wet.

Six uniformed soldiers carried the remains of André Malraux on their shoulders. They marched in step down the square with the heavy coffin. Inside the box there must have been only bones. The corpse had been exhumed for this moment.

The term ended and I went back to my home in British Columbia. In the Vancouver airport I was picked up by my friend Imogen. She was there in her black and white checkered coat and curly brown hair. We took my suitcases to the car. It was my own Jeep, which Imogen kept for me in Vancouver. As we drove to her house, she told me she had just read a book by Joseph H. Berke titled *The Tyranny of Malice*. She wanted me to borrow the book. It was about envy. About malice.

We had pasta with pesto sauce and a little wine. After, I took the book and the Jeep and headed out to Horseshoe Bay. It was the last ferry. Very few people waited to board. On the way across the sound, I fell asleep. When I arrived at my house, the place was cold. It was so evident no one had been there for at least six weeks. A lonely feeling.

I knew then that I loved my home and I did not love it. My reasons for moving into the country, away from everything, were still unclear to me. I did not know what I was trying to avoid by being so out of reach. Out of curiosity, I began to read Imogen's book. In it, Berke claims that envy, once aroused, is sadistic and malicious. The envied person is affected by the begrudging of the envier. The envier can actually alter the victim's responses to the world. He cites the case of Othello and Iago. How Iago alters not only Othello's perception but his whole psychology by his envious actions.

The envied one knows this. There is an attempt to escape. *The wish to escape from the envier*, Berke writes, *whether real or imagined, external or internal, leads the envied person to have an extreme sensitivity to the malevolent intentions of others. All his senses may be constantly attuned to detecting shafts of hatred and misfortune emanating from inanimate as well as human sources.*

It is this phenomenon that explains what is known as a fear of success. The fear of rousing envy. The fear of receiving compliments. Because it is dangerous.

The worst thing that can happen, he said to me on the phone, *is that someone dies from this.* I was looking out into the empty space that should have been the water of the fjord. Instead the falling snow shrouded the view. Nothing was visible except the dark air and the golf-ball-sized snowflakes lightly sailing down.

I was snowed in. The snow was wet and slippery. It was not possible to drive down the hillside and make the turn at the bottom without ending up in the forest below. Among the tall cedars, perhaps upside down in the Jeep. So I waited at home. Perhaps the weather would warm and the snow turn to rain. But the snow fell all day and all night. In the morning I saw the paw prints of some large animal, a cougar perhaps, threading its way from one end of my yard to the other. The path of the cougar cut a straight line just below my bedroom window.

I watched my colleague Jeremy unpack his diabetic kit. He took out a small vial of clear liquid, a wad of gauze, and one of the disposable needles. His slightly balding head, I noticed, actually suited him. His straight nose and clear eyes made him look focused. His face betrayed no expression. *I didn't know you were diabetic*, I said to him. He did not look up. *I'm not*, he countered. *Then what's this stuff?* I asked. *Isn't it insulin?*

He shook his head slightly. With his glasses on, he was filling the plastic compartment on the needle with the transparent solution. *And this isn't for me*, he corrected me. *This is my solution for you.*

My dear Jan. There was so much I could not have told him anyway. Imposing silence and secrecy made no difference after all. It was obvious to me that when two people communicate, most of what they wish to say is lost in the transaction.

There were not many ways to avoid feeling pain. Just a

few. From my reading, I could tell how some release their pain by transferring it to others. Some internalize the pain and suffer immensely. For me there was a way after all. Just numb it. I found it did not hurt at all. Just a moment, while the needle went through.

It was not something I would have wanted to tell him anyway. How I simply let it happen. The way I had let everything happen this time. Let my life wash over me without trying to control it. At first it seemed of no consequence. Jeremy and I continued to talk about work, colleagues, the weather. About ourselves and the books we read. I stood up to go home. It was getting late.

On my way to the front door, I stopped. Standing in the middle of the floor, I noticed the room was going through changes.

How do you translate the silence of the real encounter between the two of us? asks Clarise Lispector.

It's so hard to speak and say things that cannot be said. So we let it go. We do not try to translate. There is no meaning to find here except in the light beating of the heart and the sweet tinge of nerves that will not go away. To read our encounter as a poem. To try not to impose meaning, but simply let it wash over.

At Christmas I went back to Copenhagen. While I was gone, my Aunt Bodil had made peace with her daughter Kari. She, in turn, had made peace with her son, Njord. My two aunts,

Trine and Bodil, who had never been close, had made peace with each other and begun to socialize together. The two sisters, Kari and Gitte, had made peace with each other as well. It was almost a shock to me when I walked into the house. I came back to a happy family.

My cousin Niels Eric was a tall, slender fellow with yellow hair. He was a gardener by trade and wanted to show me the gardens at Frederiksborg Castle. We drove through the tiny Danish villages with crooked roads meandering through and straw-thatched houses made of stone, bracketed by wooden borders. There was a thin layer of frost everywhere and haze in the air. When Niels Eric spoke, his voice was subdued and he seemed to mumble. It was the dialect of inner Copenhagen and I was not used to it. He had a scar on his chin from an accident at work and wide open, blue eyes.

We parked at a village roadside and walked onto the castle grounds. The sun was low in the sky and the haze shrouded the light. The castle towers stood in silhouette against the orange sun. Around the towering building was a wide moat, and the water in it was lead gray. In December, when the leaves were gone, the pruned linden trees stood crooked and knobbly like sentinels from death. The walks along those denuded trunks were eerie. Something out of a dangerous tale.

After a while I found myself freezing cold. The black leather boots and brown felt coat that somehow kept me warm on the Canadian prairie at thirty below were suddenly far too thin and flimsy in the Danish winter frost. The climate was much milder in Denmark, but strangely much colder. The cold penetrated my bones and my feet ached.

We went into the castle, thinking perhaps we could warm up inside. The fortress was a labyrinth of rooms. We repeatedly got lost wandering from room to room. Each room had several doors in all directions and there were no hallways. The building was very cold, and I did not get rid of the chill in my bones. I wandered around inside the labyrinthine castle, shivering. Everywhere overhead hung portraits in oil of Danish aristocrats. They all wore wigs and were overweight and ugly. They must have been short people because the beds looked like they were meant for children. Later I learned they slept sitting up in them.

Niels Eric told me that Frederiksborg Castle had once been gutted by fire and had to be rebuilt inside. It happened because the king was so cold that he ordered fires to be lit in all the fireplaces. In every room the fires were going, and the whole castle burned down. When they rebuilt, radiators were installed. A mild warmth issued from them where they stood under the huge windows. I went up to one of the radiators to get warmed up. With my cold hands on the heater, I stood and looked out the window at the grounds we had just come through. The surreal linden trees towered beyond. The tiny village beside the grounds could be seen between the huge trunks. Yellow stuccoed farmhouses and silver-frosted grass. I felt at home.

Fantasy is a place where it rains, asserts Italo Calvino in *Six Memos for the Next Millenium.* He is talking about Dante's *Purgatorio.* The poet is in the circle of the Wrathful and has a myriad of images form in his mind. *He realizes that these images rain down from the heavens.*

I was trying to remember what freedom was like. The personal freedom that had taken so many years to perfect. How I had thrown it all away because of love. Not mild or gentle, but mad. A mad and violent love that made me desperate. How I lost myself.

In the early morning, the sky still black over my university city, I looked at the lights glinting in the distance. The occasional spot of yellow that moved in the sky to say an airplane was coming in or leaving. The cold frost on the streets. Eddies of old snow fanning in circles at corners.

I was thinking about spring. My home in the hills above the Pacific Ocean. About going home and closing the door. Secure in myself.

In the center of Oslo there was a high fashion boutique by the name of Désirée. The haute couture shop was on the corner of a slick part of downtown. Cars drove past on the avenue and slowed down at Désirée's corner. The windows displayed a row of full-sized mannequins in elegant attire. It was

December. All the mannequins were garbed in shiny, ruby red dresses. Some had black vests or black shoes or little black jackets, but all the dresses were bright red.

It was rumored in Oslo that the owner of Désirée was the king's mistress. That sometimes at night, a limousine pulled up to her door and then drove her to the palace at the end of Karl Johan Street. There, Norway's solitary king waited.

It's time now, he said to me over the phone. *We can't put it off any longer. We need to be together.*

I picked up my airplane ticket at the post office in Caen, in France. A pleasant man behind the counter rolled a cylinder into the wall, and after a minute the cylinder rolled back with my ticket inside. On the way back from the post office, the streets of Caen became congested around the stadium. A hockey game was about to start. The taxi driver picked up his wife on the way. She seated herself in the front beside him. Her hair was newly shaped and lacquered. Her face was painted and her nails were stark red.

We crawled through the tight Normandy streets. I was thinking to myself in the back seat. Who was this man in Oslo who could tell me to wait and I waited? Who told me to come to him and I went? As I sat quietly in the back, looking at the passing antique shops and lingerie boutiques and cafés, it seemed to me I was hypnotized.

I sent a black velvet dress ahead of me in the post. It was a simple, ankle-length affair, with long sleeves and high collar. It was not clear to me the occasion would ever arise when I would wear the dress. But he kept it for me. In the end I did put it on. It was to see Puccini's *Tosca* at the old Oslo Opera House.

In the first act of *Tosca*, the two lovers are introduced and flirt their way through to the end. In the second act, he is tortured and then she is tortured. The torture lasts to the end. In the third act, he is jailed, she commits murder, he is executed, and then she is executed.

When I arrived at the train station in St. Lazarre in Paris, it was already dark. A heavy rain fell and an icy wind blew. The damp chill penetrated my brown felt coat. I tried to figure out which train went to Caen. It was not obvious to me.

The station was dark and damp. Debris lay about the concrete floor. Some mad people wandered aimlessly, mumbling. The entrance to the tracks was open to the wind that welled through. People stood in stony silence, faces intense, shoulders hunched forward. They crowded around the board that displayed track numbers. As soon as a new number appeared, they raced madly to the train. The sound they made rushing forward was thick and furry. Overhead, heavy pigeons flapped across the open spaces under the ceiling.

The family was assembled for a late holiday dinner. We were in my Aunt Trine's log house in the countryside, near the village of Kregme in northern Sjælland. The long table stretched from the dining room into the kitchen. Food went around and wine was poured. All my aunts and uncles and cousins and cousins' children were talking like a happy family. I had been so cold when we were out walking earlier in the day, and the food warmed me up.

It seemed to me they were beginning to understand that I was returning. That I would be a presence at these gatherings from this year on. They were not sure what to make of it. They did not ask many questions. Niels Eric sat opposite me across the wooden table. He kept returning his attention to me, as if there was something he was about to say.

I told them I was going to Norway to see my lover. That he had sent me this ticket when I was in France. Niels Eric's sport was hiking, and he said he often went to Norway to wander in the mountains. He had a mischievous look on his face. His short yellow hair appeared matte in the low light of the room. *You know*, he said, *if you put a roof over Norway, it would be one long church.*

When we walked into his house in Oslo, he presented me with a gift. It was a gold chain with a gold pendant on it. Two loose ends were connected around a small, bright ruby.

When I was fourteen, I was confirmed in a small, wooden church. My family banded together and gave me a gold cross on a gold chain. I put the cross on around my neck and never took it off again.

Now I took the cross off for the first time. I put the small, red ruby around my neck instead. *I have a new mythology*, I said to him.

The rose is the feminine flower, writes Clarise Lispector, *that gives of itself all and so completely that the only joy left to it is to have given itself.*

All day I tried to understand. How I removed myself from my life and then longed for my life back. I knew I could take it back any time. Nothing went away. My work, my friends, my home, my family. They were all there. It was I who was no longer there. Everything was up to me.

The days passed slowly. I did not go to the office. Instead I took my work home. The afternoon lingered, sunshine coming in the window. The weather warmed. Small drops fell from the balcony above. I tried to concentrate, but my mind was elsewhere. I could not help thinking that if you give yourself away, you want to know you have not thrown yourself away.

Through the window of the small airplane, the floodplain that is Denmark receded on the left while the jagged edges of the Scandinavian peninsula appeared on the right. So close. I left my cousin Gitte's husband, Harry, at the airport in Kastrup, Copenhagen, and boarded the flight for Fornebu at Oslo. Harry could not help carry my bag because of a bad back. But somehow we got it to the check-in. Now I was taking the last leg of a long journey. My lover was in Fornebu airport waiting behind those glass doors.

I could tell I was nervous. I had not seen him for months. Months of silence and desperation. Always the promise this day would come, and the fear it never would. The counting of days. The staring at the silent telephone. The days of doubt, when I had given him up for lost. The way you do with relatives gone to war, whom you do not hear from anymore. The sense that something unsayable has happened. Someone has died. And yet the day came. Inexplicably the airplane began its descent over Oslofjorden.

The department I worked in was divided between two factions: the conservatives and the radicals. The conservatives wanted traditional teaching and traditional texts. The radicals wanted innovative teaching and nontraditional texts. The conservatives wanted to strictly safeguard the field. The radicals wanted to involve all sorts of other disciplines.

My colleague Jeremy was in the forefront of the conservatives. He was in a gang that called themselves merit only, which meant they were against affirmative action. I was grouped among the radicals. One of the post-modernists, which meant I knew no bounds. These two factions were not on speaking terms. Hateful polemics sometimes appeared in the university and city media, one side pitted against the other and townspeople generally siding with the conservatives. Some arguments between members of the different factions ended up in a call for lawyers or in resignations. There was always character assassination involved.

For this reason it was highly unorthodox that I should

find myself in Jeremy's apartment. Theoretically we should never be friends. For us to be together was like crossing over from the West side to the East side, or from the East side to the West side. A sense of betrayal was in the air.

It occurred to me I should be careful with my Karma. That my Karma remained much the same as it was ten years ago. Something always interfered with my plans to abdicate my own life. It was never in the books that I should be allowed to give myself over and try to live on another's agenda. I was forced back to my own track. It seemed to me an ominous record, and I would be a fool to disregard the evidence. That the only way to prevent the chaos of taking a wrong turn was to realize my fate and stick to it.

Or perhaps that was what my Karma was actually made of. My sense of doom when it came to my own happiness. That I would not forge ahead because I thought I should have to pay for it. Pay for my own happiness. That happiness was not something I could expect. It would never come to me. I could not help wondering how it was possible to know these things. What was the truth about fate?

There is a suspicion that the world unfolds according to your own expectations.

My dear Jan. In every greeting there is a hidden farewell. Because we have been apart long enough to require a greeting, there is the understanding we will be apart again.

Something in his story did not wash. No matter how hard I tried to reason out the circumstances, the story could not come clean. I became weary of taking his side. Of blaming others for what was happening to him. The idea that we are responsible for ourselves took hold of me.

It was the first time I had ever been upset at him. Before this, my blinding love clouded all perspective. Perhaps this was a sign that I was awakening. That he was losing his power over me. That I wanted to awaken. The dreams that beset me had become bad dreams.

But the daylight I woke to was bitter and cold. The radio announced it was minus thirty-four. However, there was a wind, so the effective temperature was minus seventy-two. They said your skin would freeze in one minute if it was exposed.

I trudged to work in the extreme cold. We had a thesis defense scheduled, something I had supervised. The examination took place in a room with big windows through which the arctic air penetrated. I had two extra sweaters with me and a box of Kleenex with which to nurse a cold. The candidate answered all the questions. He proved himself intellectually competent and well read. So I took him and the committee to the Highlevel Diner for lunch when it was over. My colleague Doug sat across from me over leek soup and told us about a friend of his in Siberia. In Siberia it got to be sixty below. When people walked along the road, you could see the trail of the swath they cut in the air. The groove in the sliced air behind them remained visible for several minutes after they were gone.

I had been back from Oslo for a week when I fell ill. It was something I might have expected. The intensity of our meeting, the sense of expectation, and then returning. Then nothing. The sky over my university city was bleak and cold. The streets were slick and frosty. I battled my condition for a week, continuing to go to work, until I gave up. Canceled everything and took myself in hand. It was a self-destructive attitude to care nothing for my health. I could not understand where this disposition came from.

For the weekend I returned to British Columbia to finish what appeared to be a good recovery. It was warm in Vancouver. The sun was shining. People were out in their shirt sleeves. The smell of wet cedar and salt sea air reminded me I was glad to be back. I knew somehow in my bones that I had been very upset. But I did not know exactly why. What about. Whatever it was, the toll was being taken.

It occurred to me only too late that I might have been wrong. I was expecting something to happen. A casualty. That we could not come to the end of our story without someone falling by the wayside. Now, when I looked around me, I could see the table, the lamp, the Kelim rug. I knew the room was spinning. I knew it was because I had allowed Jeremy to put that needle in my arm. But it had not occurred to me till that moment that the casualty was me. It would be me.

That I had walked into a trap I could not get out of. The walls were moving toward me. The floor was rising at me. I could see the door from where I stood. It was the door I was heading toward. A large, brown door without a threshold. On the other side was a hallway and an elevator. I would go down the lift and out to the sidewalk. The early night air would be crisp. The river on my left. I could go down to the river along the walking trail. The snow would be crusty and old under my shoes. But my feet were not moving.

In those few moments of what seemed like extreme clarity, all of Oslo returned itself to me. I remembered clearly that Oslo did not have many faces. It was the dark time of year. Daylight came late and night arrived early. In between, the sky was overcast and the clouds were tin-colored. The air was humid. In the winter cold, hoarfrost settled everywhere. The barren trees were layered in a coat of rime. In the park in Bygdøy there was a sculpture of a nude, life-sized man. He was lying down on his right side in the snow. With a white coat of hoarfrost patched on him everywhere, it was hard to tell this was not the corpse of an unfortunate wanderer.

In the building that had been erected to house all of Edvard Munch's paintings, pride of place was given to a canvas titled *The Sick Child*. It was a painting of a young girl sitting on the edge of a bed and a woman administering to her. The girl had yellow hair and a pale face. Her expression, looking up in profile, was angelic. The painter had written about the picture, *This is not just a painting of my dying sister. This is everyone I have ever lost.*

Almost everyone in Edvard Munch's family died before the age of thirty. Those who were not dead yet were coughing. It was the inheritance of tuberculosis. A ghost that would not vanish.

Munch's most famous painting, *The Scream*, was stolen. The news flash went out all over the world. *The Scream* had been stolen.

South of Oslo is a series of small villages. One of them is called Berger, once a factory village. The industry was shut down now. The large, red brick factory in the center of the village, where they used to make blankets, was abandoned. Artists had moved in. Outside the door was a life-sized sculpture by the local sculptor, Marit Wiklund, of a nude man standing, gesticulating. His body was dented all over, as if he had been severely beaten.

Below were streets lined with rows of identical wooden shacks. Small, white row houses, which were factory workers' quarters before, were now lived in by others. It was dark and the streetlights were few and dim. The streets at night were empty corridors. No one was about. It seemed to me just then that it was easy to imagine being poor.

It had been so long. I was afraid my memory deceived me. That the man I remembered, the one I had written to, spoken with, waited with, waited for, was different. That the one I canceled myself for was not the one I remembered.

I had on the brown velvet jacket from France. I told him he should look for the jacket in case I too was different. It had been so long. While I waited for the baggage to come out onto the conveyor belt, I could sense that strange, vacant feeling that comes when a flood of emotions proves too much for the limited brain. One feeling canceled out the other. Instead of a weakness in the knees, I had the kind of energy that is peculiar to soldiers heading for the front lines. I took my blue bag and walked toward the glass doors. I knew he was there on the other side of the glass. I went through.

Oslo is the world's largest village, my cousin Niels Eric claimed during dinner at my Aunt Trine's cabin near Kregme. He was joking. Everyone around the long, wooden table laughed. I disregarded his remark. The Scandinavians, I knew, were always making fun of one another. But when I came to Oslo and began living there, I discovered Niels Eric's joke had a ring of truth. That with the exception of the downtown core, all the Oslo neighborhoods were like villages. There were village streets, village corner groceries, village houses made of wood, and village neighbors.

The basement apartment that was to be my home was very small. It was the bottom floor of a single-story house. There were only two rooms, both overheated, condensation forming along the windows. The kitchen was only a corner of the single room where everything went on. Old and faded furniture lined the place. We did not notice. We spent our days and nights in each other's arms.

It was something I had not thought myself capable of. That I would exchange my life of luxury, an estate by the sea in British Columbia, a desirable university job, for a life of poverty among the hills of southern Norway. Where the water in the fjord froze every winter. Where the damp cold penetrated the wooden walls. Where we had to search the lining of our coat pockets to find loose change so we could get a bit of herring. It had appeared to me finally, after all this time, that love was the only thing that counted. After love, the love you have for another, everything else falls away. Everything else is unimportant.

The night was dark. Almost no streetlights could be seen. We slept in each other's arms in the small bedroom. Tightly together, we would not let each other go.

I awoke to the sound of his voice. He was asleep but his lips were parted. It was a nightmare. He screamed. He was trying to wake himself up from the horrible dream, so he screamed.

Dear, dear Jan. We came to a place where my words could finally reach him. We could send our words over the wire. We could talk on the telephone. The white phone in my living room showed signs of use. A darker band where my hand gripped the receiver. The sweat of my palm because there was always some level of agitation. That we were always too far away from each other. Being together only made the later, inevitable separation worse.

And yet I wanted my freedom. My desire to be free lingered, like the remnants of a disease you cannot quite recover from. *And that's why I sense we shall soon separate,* writes Clarise Lispector. *My astonishing truth is that I was always alone, separate from you, and I didn't know it. Now I know; I'm alone. I and my freedom.*

It was a winter that would not go away. In the middle of March, it was still twenty-one below. Snow was still falling. Roofs of houses had snow piled high. Streets remained impassable. On election day in Alberta, there was a blizzard. City streets had not been cleared because of government spending cutbacks. People risked their lives behind the wheel. Only fifty-seven percent of the populace made it to the polls, and they re-elected the Tories. This way we could be sure the streets would remain unsafe for the next four years.

I did not tell my lover directly what I was thinking, but he knew. It was apparent to him across the distance between us that I was withdrawing. It was a psychic withdrawal. An emotional fading. He said he could hear it in the tone of my voice. That I had begun to whisper. That he was determined to persuade me to stay with him. To return to him.

Two days later he was on a British Airways flight that landed in Vancouver at five in the evening. I promised to be there and to take him to my home in the mountains. The home I wanted to keep for my own life. As I waited in the new wing of the Vancouver Airport, I thought of the words of Clarise Lispector. What she said about the life I wanted for myself. *Yes, life is very oriental,* she wrote. She talked about *the elusive and delicate freedom of life. It's like knowing how to arrange flowers in a vase; an almost useless skill.*

Because I went home, to my retreat in British Columbia, to think. To ask myself the important questions. The big questions. As it happened, it was Valentine's Day. At ten in the morning on the fourteenth of February, a dark-haired woman knocked on my door. She was holding a bouquet of flowers. She delivered the flowers to me and said she was from Anne Lynn's flower shop in the village. I took the bouquet and read the card. It was from my lover. He was trying to win me over again.

I did not have a vase, so I took down an old pewter coffee pot. The pot had belonged to my mother, who got it from her father, who got it from his ancestors. The pot originated on the Jylland peninsula. Now it stood on the railing of the landing in my house. Out of this small ancestral inheritance, my lover's live spray of tiger lilies, carnations, roses, and daisies burst open.

I began to gather strength. This time I could tell I was much more successful. I altered my thinking. Put on men's clothes. Jeans and men's shirts, striped suits and ties. I invited my friend Linda to come to my house in the mountains for three days. Linda was getting a divorce. I said to her we should celebrate her divorce, which happened to fall on Valentine's Day. Three days before my lover flew in from London.

The only restaurant with a free table on February fourteenth was Lord Jim's Resort, sixty kilometers north on the coast. Linda and I drove through the black rain, turned off the highway, and wound our way to the resort through the dense forest. It was a log cabin by the sea. We walked in, my black suit five sizes too large, so the sleeves hung out over my hands and the pants bunched up at the bottom. But I was feeling careless.

Linda and I turned out to be the only same-sex couple in the place. They were trying to serve haute cuisine that evening. Nouveau cuisine at Lord Jim's consisted of simply putting very little food on the plate. During dinner a woman in high heels went around to all the tables offering a long-stemmed rose to the lady. When she came to our table, she stood there lost, holding the bright red rose. She looked from one to the other and did not know which one of us to give the flower to.

So I think that once we are no longer little children, it is really up to us to show a certain poise, and stride out into the space provided for us, Christa Wolf said in an interview. Now it seemed to me that it was useless to do anything else. To be courageous, to face what there was. Not to flinch. Not to complain. And I had made my decisions. To stand on my ground. Not to give myself away.

So I stood at the Vancouver International Airport. It was the new terminal with the green sculpture by Bill Reid. Of a canoe full of creatures. The sculpture said we are all packed in the same canoe together. We cannot escape. In my long, navy, pinstriped suit jacket, I paced the gleaming floors. I sat down and read the *Globe and Mail* cover to cover. Then the *Vancouver Sun.* A kind of peace had descended on me.

Eventually they let the passengers out of the British Airways flight from London. One by one they came through the glass doors and strode down the long passageway.

The unseasonable cold lay over all of Canada. It was at that time that I went on a business trip to Saskatoon. From cold city to cold city. At the Ramada Inn, where I was put, the American rooms were large with big beds in them. Downstairs in the huge foyer, people in jeans and cowboy hats and big winter parkas ran in and out energetically. I unpacked in the room and went out for a walk. There was a brisk wind. Snow was everywhere. I chanced into a shop that was selling everything at nearly a hundred percent discount, so I bought a red shirt. It was blood red.

Next morning I made coffee in the room with the machine provided. It was a pale, icy morning. I put on the blood-red shirt and drank the coffee. Settled in to read a book of interviews with Christa Wolf. It occurred to me that I was strangely happy. Even though it was only yesterday I was so agitated. Yesterday I wept over what lay between me and my lover. Today I was strangely happy. I did not understand my own happiness.

The poet Tim Lillburn picked me up at the Saskatoon airport. He was a little rounder than I remembered him. He had on a white jacket and white trousers, padded on the inside, and a fur hat. We went out to lunch. Tim had a glass of Australian Shiraz and we talked about wine. About living in rural Saskatchewan in houses that cost only a thousand dollars.

In the evening several of us were gathered in a Vietnamese restaurant where we spent a long time talking and sampling what appeared to be an endless number of dishes continually appearing. Afterward we all went in different directions. As I got into my friends' car, I looked down the street where Tim was walking away by himself. It was a lonely, white-clad figure that walked away from us in the snow.

The floor in Jeremy's apartment rose to meet me. I knew what was going on. It was clear to me I had allowed this to happen. It was also obvious to me that what I had done would have to take its course. I could not turn the clock back. We could not even go back the twenty minutes or so since my colleague Jeremy had put the needle into my arm. He said I would feel better. He said I would forget my pain. The illness of uncertainty and fear my lover had caused. The apprehension someone was being harmed. And that person must be me. It rang like a siren in my ear that it must be me. The light in the distant darkness that signaled an oncoming train.

It was the dead of night. The sky was pitch black. The ocean water below the floor was coal black. Our house was made of wood and shaped like an octagon. It was a houseboat because it floated on the water, tied lightly to the pier. He and I, my lover and I, were inside. We were seated at a small, round table. Perhaps we were having dinner. There was a child with us. I did not remember if the child was his, or mine, or one we had together.

We looked out the window into the south. Just then a train sped into view. I said happily to the child, "Look, a water-train." Because it was a sleek, yellow train that ran on the water like a hydrofoil. The train went very fast. Just outside our houseboat, the water-train made a sharp turn. All the wagons behind the engine ended up banging sideways into the platform of our house. We felt the reverberations like heavy earthquakes. The whole house veered and jolted with each wagon that hit. The house came loose from its moorings.

Just when I thought it was over and the train would continue, the engine turned toward us. The front light shone starkly into the dark interior of the house. A big clip in front of the train took hold of the deck of the house and began to push us. It dawned on me, only too late, that the train was taking us away. The whole house and everything in it. The three of us, surprised inside. The yellow water-train sped off into the darkest night, carrying us three in its mouth.

My dear Jan. I put down the book by Clarise Lispector I have been reading all along. *The Stream of Life.* It is a short book, only seventy pages. It is chaotic and formless. There is no pattern or development. She says her writing is *a night passed entirely on a back road where no one is.* She says her story is *of roots dormant in their strength.*

It is that strength I find myself drawing from. I wonder at her, that other woman, who gave something of herself I could take, so long after. It was something she wrote in between. While sitting on a warm verandah, a cigarette smoking itself in the ashtray. She had moments of happiness. *I'm being happy,* she wrote, *because I refuse to be vanquished.* But more: *therefore I love,* she says. *That's happiness: even love that doesn't work out, even love that ends.*

To be free, says Toni Morrison in her little book *Playing in the Dark*, is also the freedom *to narrate the world*. To say what is. To be in my own story and not someone else's. That is what I saw in Clarise Lispector's book. She seized her own story and held it. The way a tiny Rufous Hummingbird holds on to the naked branch below. The branch stands straight into the sky without leaves, and on the very tip is a red-throated hummingbird, ticking for a new aerial display. It is his desire to fling straight up and then throw himself down at breakneck speed.

I know it is not an easy flight he is about to make. But he will. I know he will.

Sources Cited

Berke, Joseph H. *The Tyranny of Malice*. New York: Summit Books, 1988.

Calvino, Italo. *Six Memos for the Next Millennium*. New York: Vintage, 1988.

Cixous, Hélène. *Coming to Writing and Other Essays*. London: Harvard University Press, 1991.

Dillard, Annie. *The Writing Life*. New York: Harper Collins, 1990.

Guterson, David. *Snow Falling on Cedars*. New York: Vintage, 1995.

Hesse, Hermann. *Steppenwolf*. Trans. Basil Creighton. New York: Henry Holt, 1963.

Lispector, Clarise. *The Stream of Life*. Trans. Elizabeth Lowe and Earl Fitz. Minneapolis: University of Minnesota Press, 1989.

Morrison, Toni. *Beloved*. New York: Signet, 1991.

——. *Playing in the Dark*. New York: Vintage, 1992.

Robbe-Grillet, Alain. *For a New Novel*. Trans. Richard Howard. Evanston: Northwestern University Press, 1965.

Welty, Eudora. *The Eye of the Story*. New York: Vintage, 1990.

Wolf, Christa. *The Fourth Dimension: Interviews with Christa Wolf*. Trans. Hilary Pilkington. London: Verso, 1988.